Stories from the Heart

John Russell

HojoPress Publications

First paperback edition August 2024

ISBN: (paperback) 979-8-9896331-8-0

ISBN: (ebook) 979-8-9896331-9-7

Book design by Durga Khatri

www.hojopresspublishing.com

To my readers,

This collection is dedicated to those who believe in the quiet power of kindness, the healing embrace of creativity, and the enduring strength of love. May these stories remind you that even in the smallest gestures, we can find connection, hope, and the courage to face life's challenges.

Thank you for sharing in this journey.

Prologue

Stories are born in the quiet corners of life, where moments pass unnoticed. These stories—woven from the threads of hope, loss, love, and resilience—echo the human spirit. *Stories from the Heart* brings these hidden tales to light, reminding us that extraordinary journeys unfold within the mundane.

At the heart of Serendipity Café, Emma, a woman shaped by life's challenges, is surrounded by the guarded glances of coworkers and the solitude sought by patrons. Yet, she harbors a quiet determination to spread kindness, even in the face of her struggles. A simple misunderstanding over a sketchbook becomes a turning point, where Emma's gentle intervention transforms tension into connection.

Inspired by this, she leaves anonymous notes of encouragement, igniting a spark of warmth and unity within the café's walls. Through her small acts of kindness, Emma reveals the profound impact one person can have on an entire community, proving that sometimes, the smallest gestures heal the deepest wounds.

In a different corner of life, Bella and James, childhood friends whose bond was once unbreakable, are torn apart by adolescence's careless whisper. The pain of betrayal lingers, turning their shared memories into a haunting reminder of lost connection. Years later, as adults navigate their artistic paths, an unexpected reunion in their hometown art gallery stirs the embers of their past. Their shared love of art becomes a bridge, offering a chance at reconciliation and healing. In *The Art of Forgiveness*, their story is a testament to the power of creativity and the courage it takes to mend what was once broken.

Clara, a gifted violinist, faces the devastating loss of both her instrument and her ability to play after a tragic accident. Her recovery journey in *The Healing of Music* is physical and emotional, as she learns to reconnect with her passion through the healing power of music. At a unique rehabilitation clinic, Clara forms an unspoken bond with Alex, a mute pianist. Together, they discover that music transcends words, and through their shared sessions, they inspire those around them. Clara's story is one of resilience, of finding new ways to express old passions, and of the healing that comes from creative connection.

In *The Gift of Time*, Scott Taylor, a man whose ambition once consumed him, finds himself at a crossroads. His relentless pursuit of success has come at the cost of his most precious relationships. A simple gift from his daughters—a homemade coupon book filled with family activities—forces Scott to confront the growing distance between him and his loved ones. This story is a reminder that time, once lost, cannot be regained, but it also highlights the power of choice in reclaiming what truly matters.

Finally, *The Last Dance* tells the story of Rose and James, a couple whose love has weathered the storms of life. Their journey from a chance meeting in a café to the twilight of their lives is marked by joy, laughter, and shared resilience. As they dance one last time in the ballroom where their love first bloomed, they celebrate a life well-lived, filled with memories that will endure beyond their final dance.

Though diverse in their characters and settings, these stories share a common thread: the resilience of the human spirit. *Stories from the Heart* invites readers to find themselves in these tales, to see their struggles and triumphs reflected in the lives of others, and to be reminded that in the smallest moments, the greatest stories are told.

Contents

Serendipity Cafe

E mma's challenges were as varied as they were formidable. She battled the lingering grief of losing her mother at a young age, a void that seemed impossible to fill. Financial struggles were a constant companion. She struggled to make ends meet while saving up for her dream - a community center.

Despite her burdens, Emma struggled to connect with others, which left a gap in her life. She felt alone, without a close confidant with whom to share her thoughts and feelings.

Yet, through it all, Emma's resolve never wavered, her heart remaining steadfast in its pursuit of spreading kindness and hope.

Emma's life bore the marks of battles and resilient moments, weathering storms that shaped her empathy and compassion. In the face of personal challenges, she possessed an innate inclination to uplift those around her, finding comfort in her relationship with her roommate, Brittany. Despite its friendliness, the relationship was characterized as coexisting roommates who respected each other's space.

This absence made her more eager to make a positive impact on others, fueling her desire to spread kindness. Without a close relationship, her need for affirmation and the chance to uplift others grew stronger.

Serendipity Café was another stop in Emma's life journey—a job to pay the bills. Having weathered personal storms and confronted numerous challenges, Emma was at a crossroads. She couldn't help but feel that her life might revolve around unremarkable work. The café was where she'd continue serving coffee, engaging in casual conversations, and witnessing transient moments without making any tangible difference. A conflict brewed within her, a struggle between her genuine desire to create meaningful change and the seeming permanence of her role.

Co-workers were guarded and friendly yet cautious when revealing their inner worlds. Friendship existed, but conversations often skirted deeper connections. The patrons, while kind, desired solitude. Many sought refuge within the café's embrace but preferred moments of respite in privacy, with polite exchanges during orders being customary. Emma respected these boundaries, acknowledging the need for privacy in the bustling café ambiance.

Lost in contemplation after each shift, Emma would return to her apartment, greeted by her roommate's familiar routine and distant presence. She would drop her keys on the counter, change out of her work clothes, and sit by the window, staring out into the night. Her aspirations clashed with the reality of her job. This desire to make a difference battled against the demands of daily life, an internal struggle that grew louder each day.

The exterior tells a tale of resilience, with aged bricks and wooden details that narrated the passage of time through their cracks and textures. Touches of greenery added vibrant contrast to the weathered façade. Inside, the café exuded a comforting ambiance with laughter, soft conversations, and the clinking of cups. The friendly baristas, who wore coffee-stained aprons and warm smiles, epitomized the café's heart of hospitality.

The café is a charming chaos of mismatched furniture draped in funky fabrics, creating cozy nooks. The tables carry the imprints of countless conversations. Our regulars aren't patrons; they're storytellers. We all gather here for warmth and great company.

Paige grabs what she thinks is her trusty dog-eared notebook. Lost in her creative bubble, she only realizes it's Gabby's cherished sketchbook when she settles into her usual spot.

Gabby discovered her beloved sketchbook was missing. Panic set in as she searched her table and then scoured the café. Her emotions, tangled up in her artwork, went into overdrive with anxiety and distress. She frantically checked her tote bag, glanced at the seats around her, and even looked at the floor. Her anxiety grew with each passing moment. Convinced someone had taken her sketchbook, Gabby's heart raced when she spotted Paige across the café. Without thinking twice, she marched over, her emotions raw and on edge.

"Paige, did you take my sketchbook?" Gabby's voice wavered, the concern in her eyes sharpening to suspicion.

Paige's eyes widened, and she stammered, "Your sketchbook? I... I don't think so. I only have my notebook with me." Her brows furrowed as she glanced around, clearly puzzled.

"You do!" Gabby's voice grew louder. She pointed at Paige's worn book.

The lively café atmosphere faded as tension thickened. Nearby conversations were hushed, and curious eyes turned toward Gabby and Paige. The clinking of coffee cups and the hum of chatter seemed to pause, amplifying the charged silence between them. Emma sensed the rising anxiety. She stepped in before emotions escalated further.

"Is everything okay here?" Emma's voice was a soothing presence amid the brewing conflict.

With emotions running high, Gabby explained, "My sketchbook... it's gone. Paige has it."

"Gabby, I think this might be a misunderstanding," She interjected, shifting her attention to Paige. "Paige, could we take a moment? Let's figure this out together."

Paige nodded, her confusion mirrored in her eyes. "I don't have Gabby's sketchbook," she reiterated.

Gabby stepped closer, her finger pointed sharply. "Yes, you do."

Paige's eyes followed Gabby's finger, landing on the sketchbook beside her coffee. She frowned, her confusion deepening. Reaching for it, Paige hesitated, then flipped it open. The pages revealed sketches she had never seen—detailed, emotional drawings unmistakably Gabby's.

Her face flushed with embarrassment as the realization dawned. "Oh, I... I didn't even notice. I'm so sorry, Gabby."

Before Gabby could respond, Emma, the café manager, stepped in. "Ladies, why don't we step over here?" she suggested gently, guiding them to a quiet corner away from the prying eyes and hushed whispers of other patrons.

As they sat down, Emma spoke softly, "Let's talk this out calmly, okay?" Paige nodded, still holding the sketchbook; her expression was a relief. Gabby seemed to relax slightly, ready to resolve the misunderstanding.

Gabby's clenched fists slowly loosened as Paige's explanation unfolded. She noticed the genuine confusion in Paige's eyes, but the thought of someone else touching her sketches left her feeling unsettled. "I'm sorry, Gabby. I never meant to take your sketchbook. It was an honest mistake," Paige apologized.

Gabby sighed, the tension in her shoulders easing slightly. Her eyes softened as she looked at the person in front of her. "I overreacted," she confessed, a hint of embarrassment coloring her cheeks. "My sketchbook holds a lot of sentimental value. I thought it was gone," she admitted, her voice now trembling with relief. She wrapped her arms around herself as if comforting her heart, feeling the weight of the misunderstanding lift.

"You both have such unique ways of expressing yourselves through your art. Paige, have you shown Gabby your writing?" said Emma.

Paige nodded, an uncertain smile forming on her lips. "No, not really."

"Maybe this could be a good moment," Emma suggested. Paige opened up about her stories, and vulnerability replaced their tension. Gabby was touched by Paige's openness and the emotional significance behind some of her sketches. Their conversation evolved from tension to understanding, strengthening their bond through mutual appreciation of their creative processes.

Some mornings, the café bustles with animated discussions among book club members. Afternoons witness the quiet contemplation of writers and artists seeking inspiration in the café's embrace. Friendships flourish, nurtured by cups of coffee and moments of vulnerability exchanged like cherished tokens.

New faces drifted in and sensed Jessica's weary posture, recognizing the weight of long shifts in her tired eyes. Her observations delved into actions. Professor Miller's habit of pausing to engage in deep discussions, understanding his need for intellectual discourse. Emma recognized the comfort Mr. Thompson found in a simple cup of tea.

She grasps this desire to help. The café becomes a canvas where hope and uncertainty collide. The air quivers with her unspoken resolve, an unformed plan brewing as she seeks to encourage each cup.

The vibrant hum faded into the background as she dialed Brittany, her roommate. She was eager to share an idea that had taken root in her mind.

"Hey, I've been thinking... What if we did something to lift everyone's spirits?" She proposed, her voice carrying the spark of a newfound plan.

Curiosity piqued, Brittany responded, "What's on your mind?"

She stared at a blank piece of paper with a pen in hand. Doubts crept into her thoughts as she wondered whether a few words on paper could make a difference. She sighed and began to write.

The first note found its way to Paige, who was grappling with the challenge of writer's block. Tucked under Paige's customary coffee cup, the note caught her eye as she stared at the daunting blank pages of her notebook. It read:

"Amidst the blank pages, your words dance like stars awaiting their constellation. It whispers stories waiting to be written. You're a creator of worlds—embrace the magic within you."

Bewildered by the unexpected message beneath her cup, Paige's surprise transformed into a faint smile. The simple words stirred something within her. Sipping her coffee, Paige found herself reflecting on the notes. They lingered like a gentle whisper, dispelling her writer's block and infusing the blank pages with the promise of unwritten stories.

Paige waved her over. "Hey Emma, can I talk to you for a second? I found this note on my cup this morning."

Emma approached the table with a warm smile and replied, "Oh, did you? Did it put a smile on your face?"

"It did more than that. I've struggled with my writing, and the messages were like a gentle push in the right direction," she responded.

"I'm glad. Whoever did it wanted to offer some encouragement," Emma reassured her.

Paige's expression reflected surprise. "They have a way with words. It's like they understand without even knowing."

Emma continued her work, wiping down a table. "Sometimes, you don't need words for what someone needs."

Paige shared her curious encounter with the unexpected message. She recounted the gentle encouragement that had rekindled her creativity.

The tale of the anonymous note found refuge in Gabby and Mr. Thompson's conversations. Their wonder at this unexpected act of kindness echoed through the café's walls.

Jessica nestled among the patrons and sat at the worn wooden counter. Though tired, her eyes were drawn to the vibrant atmosphere.

Emma welcomed her with a warm smile. "Hi. Your favorite brew today?"

She responded with a faint smile. "Yes, please. It's been quite a day."

Emma started on Jessica's coffee. "I hope things ease up for you."

She nodded. "It's been challenging, but your café is my respite. The notes, Emma... are like a breath of fresh air in chaos."

She placed the steaming coffee cup before Jessica, a note tucked beneath it. "I'm glad they bring a bit of calm. Take a moment for yourself. You deserve it," she suggested.

Jessica's gaze shifted from Emma's caring eyes to the cup and the note underneath, a sudden softness enveloping her expression. The note read:

"Remember to take it one step at a time. You are stronger than you think, and brighter days are ahead."

Jessica's eyes softened as she read the words. She had a small smile. She tucked the note into her pocket, feeling a touch of warmth and encouragement to carry her through the rest of the day.

Paige mused, "Has anyone else discovered those intriguing notes on their coffee cups? It's quite mysterious."

"I received one," Jessica announced, a subtle excitement infusing her tired voice with newfound energy.

Gabby's warm smile added a glow, saying, "Oh yes, I found one yesterday! A little quote made me smile."

Mr. Thompson, his gaze meandering through the corridors of distant memories, joined in, "Aye, I found one, too. Reminded me of my travels, it did."

Bewildered yet touched, Jessica added, "I wonder who's behind it? It's such a sweet and thoughtful gesture."

With his infectious smile spreading, Tom stated, "Probably one of the baristas, trying to brighten our days, huh?"

"Whoever it is," Professor Miller commented, "they've certainly stirred curiosity among us. It adds a touch of magic to our little community here."

Customer conversations of excitement and curiosity were in the café. Speculations about the anonymous notes created an air of intrigue, enveloping the regulars in a collective marvel at the unexpected warmth infused into their daily rituals. An undercurrent of anticipation hummed through the bustling space, prompting patrons to question the baristas. In unison, the baristas denied involvement in the notes' mysterious origins.

Amidst the lively atmosphere, Emma's thoughts were clouded with doubt about the impact of her notes. However, when she spotted Jessica across the room, eagerly sharing the notes with a group of friends, Emma's doubts began to dissipate. Jessica's animated gestures and the smiles on her friends' faces reassured her that her efforts were indeed meaningful.

Jessica noticed a note tucked underneath as she picked up her coffee cup. Her eyes widened in surprise as she read the message, a gentle smile curling her lips. She approached the counter and asked, "Emma, have you seen these notes?"

Emma met Jessica's gaze, nerves and hope mingling in her eyes. "I might know something about them," she admitted softly. Jessica's expression warmed a subtle light in her tired eyes. "Whoever wrote these has a gift for saying what people need to hear."

Emma's heart swelled with relief and gratitude. "I hoped they'd make a difference," she said. Her eyes were shining, and her vulnerability was evident in her tone. She sipped her coffee, and her demeanor changed. The weariness seemed to lift, replaced by a glimmer of renewed energy.

"These notes are like a burst of sunshine on a cloudy day," Jessica shared. "They're reminding me that small kindnesses' power in a world is too heavy."

Emma smiled. "That's exactly what I was going for," she said, contentment filling her heart. She returned to her table. Emma felt fulfilled, knowing her small gestures had brightened someone's day. The café now buzzed with newfound warmth, the notes creating connections among its patrons. Emma's journey intertwined with those she sought to uplift through interconnected stories within the walls of Serendipity Café.

"Hello, everyone," she began, her voice steady yet filled with emotion. "I wanted to share something with you all. Those little notes you find around the café are from me. I never imagined how some words on a paper could lead to so many good things."

Emma walked to the middle of the café. "I wanted to share something with you all. Those little notes you find around the café are from me. I never imagined how some words on paper could lead to so many good things—strangers smiling at each other, people paying for someone else's coffee, and heartfelt conversations that wouldn't have happened otherwise."

The patrons murmured with surprise and curiosity. Emma continued, "I've faced many challenges in my life—struggles and setbacks that sometimes felt overwhelming. But along the way, I've learned the power of small gestures. A simple word, a caring note, can make a difference."

She paused, her eyes scanning the room, connecting with each person. "There were days when a kind word or a small act of kindness from someone brightened my day and gave me hope. Those experiences inspired me to leave these notes here, in the café. I wanted to create moments of light for others, just as they were created for me."

The patrons listened intently, some nodding, others wiping away tears. Emma's voice softened as she recounted her transformative journey. "This café became more than just a place to work—it became a sanctuary for me, a haven where I could find purpose. Each note I write is a reminder that we all have the power to make a positive difference in someone's life, no matter how small the gesture."

The room was silent momentarily. Then, a wave of appreciation and admiration washed over the café.

"You've created something beautiful here," Paige approached Emma, eyes glistening with tears.

Emma smiled, her heart full. The café, now resonating with an aura of humanity and empathy, had become a haven for her and everyone who walked through its doors.

Laughter and heart-to-heart chats filled the air as familiar faces and new friends joined in a spirit of unity and gratitude. The café, adorned with colorful decorations and twinkling lights, buzzed with stories and appreciation.

Bright streamers and paper lanterns hung from the ceiling, casting a warm, festive glow. The scent of fresh coffee and baked goods mingled with the laughter, creating a cozy and celebratory atmosphere. In one corner, friends shared stories from their week, their faces animated with joy and excitement. In another, a young couple held hands, speaking in hushed tones, their eyes only for each other.

Emma was at the center of it all, moving gracefully from table to table, her presence a source of comfort and warmth. She greeted everyone with a genuine smile, her eyes sparkling with the same light as the decorations around her. She listened intently to each person, her empathy and kindness shining through in every interaction.

Near the window, an elderly man and a young girl sat side by side, the generational gap bridged by their shared laughter. The girl held a crayon, drawing pictures on a napkin, while the man recounted tales of his youth. Their bond, forged in the welcoming ambiance of the café, exemplified the spirit of unity that permeated the room.

The sound of clinking cups and the gentle hum of conversation created a soothing backdrop. Each person in the café felt a part of something larger, a community woven together by shared experiences and mutual appreciation. The café had transformed into a haven of connection, where every smile and every word added to human warmth.

The flickering lights seemed to dance in harmony with the joyous spirit of the gathering. People who had come in as strangers left with new friends, their hearts light and their spirits lifted. The café, with its colorful decorations and heartfelt conversations, had become a beacon of unity and gratitude, a place where stories were shared and memories were made.

Laughter and heart-to-heart chats filled the air as familiar faces and new friends joined in a spirit of unity and gratitude. The café buzzed with stories and appreciation.

Emma, the driving force behind the café's transformation, stood at the center, surrounded by smiles and thankful looks. Her down-to-earth vibe exuded contentment, and she absorbed the collective joy filling the space.

Expressions of thanks and recognition echoed, with patrons acknowledging the positive impacts of small acts of kindness. Stories flowed about personal growth, rekindled connections, and the profound effect of the café's compassionate atmosphere.

In this celebration, Serendipity Café stood as a physical space for the lasting power of small acts of love and the unexpected connections formed through them. It became a beacon of hope and inspiration, showcasing the profound impact of gentleness in fostering unity, healing wounds, and nurturing a sense of belonging within a community.

Weeks passed after Emma revealed the secret. The café buzzed with renewed energy daily, where hearts connected and lives intertwined.

The aroma of freshly brewed coffee filled the air one crisp morning. Emma moved behind the counter with practiced ease. The sun streamed through the windows, casting a warm glow over the café. The morning rush had begun, and Emma greeted each patron with a genuine smile, her kind words setting a positive tone for their day.

Paige approached the counter with a warm smile.

"Emma," Paige began, her voice soft but steady. "I wanted to thank you."

Emma paused and looked up from the espresso machine. "Thank me?" she asked.

Paige nodded, her smile widening. "Yes, your notes inspired me to finish my novel. I never thought a few words could mean so much."

Emma's hazel eyes sparkled with joy. She reached out and gently squeezed Paige's hand. "I'm so happy to hear that, Paige. Your novel must be amazing."

"It is," Paige replied, her voice filled with newfound confidence. "And I couldn't have done it without your encouragement. Those little notes reminded me that someone believed in me, even when I doubted myself."

Emma's heart swelled with pride. The café had become a shelter where struggles were acknowledged and celebrated. She glanced around the room, seeing familiar faces and new ones, all finding comfort and connection within the café's walls.

At a nearby table, an elderly couple shared a quiet conversation, their hands entwined. Across the room, students laughed and chatted, their textbooks spread out before them. Each person in the café contributed to the stories and experiences.

Emma turned back to Paige, her smile unwavering. "Paige, your words also mean a lot to me. It reminds me why I started leaving those notes in the first place."

Paige's eyes glistened with emotion. "Thank you, Emma. You've created something extraordinary here."

The lively Gabby sat sipping her coffee, her eyes sparkling excitedly as she looked around at the animated atmosphere. A paintbrush twirled in her fingers, a splash of vibrant color already smeared on her cheek from a recent art project.

Emma approached Gabby's table with a fresh pot of coffee, ready to offer a refill. "How's the painting coming along, Gabby?" she asked, her tone cheerful and inviting.

Gabby beamed up at her. "It's going great," she exclaimed, waving her paintbrush for emphasis.

Emma's face lit up with a smile, touched by Gabby's words. "That is wonderful."

Gabby set her brush down and sipped her coffee, her eyes dancing excitedly. "Seriously, Emma. Every time I walk in here and see those little notes, it's like a burst of inspiration. This café isn't just a place to drink coffee. You've created a space where people feel seen and heard."

Emma's heart swelled with pride and gratitude. "That's exactly what I hoped for, Gabby. To create a place where people can find comfort and connection."

Gabby nodded enthusiastically. "You've done that and more. Look around—everyone here is engaged in deep conversations, sharing parts of themselves they might not share anywhere else. It's beautiful."

As Emma glanced around the café, she saw it through Gabby's eyes. Jessica and Mr. Thompson were still deep in conversation.

She turned back to Gabby, her smile unwavering. "It's people like you who bring this place to life. Thank you."

Gabby grinned, lifting her coffee cup in a toast. "To the Serendipity Café and the magic of Emma's notes!"

The café hummed with conversations beyond the usual chatter, with each word, smile, and note brightening the day. Serendipity Café had transformed into a sanctuary where life's complexities were met with warmth, understanding, and the simple, profound act of listening. Emma realized she didn't need to open a community center to make a difference—she was already doing it right here.

The soft chime of the doorbell rang out, drawing Emma's attention from wiping down the counter. Her hands stilled as she saw an unexpected guest enter Serendipity Café. It was a local newspaper reporter known for capturing the essence of the human spirit in their articles.

"Good morning," the editor exclaimed warmly, their eyes sweeping over the welcoming atmosphere of the café. "I've heard about the incredible transformation here. Your story is nothing short of inspiring. The way this café has become a haven of kindness and connection has caught my attention. I'd love to feature you and Serendipity Café in an upcoming article for the local newspaper. What do you think?"

Emma paused. This unexpected turn of events added a new chapter that could amplify its impact on the community in ways she hadn't imagined.

The editor continued, their enthusiasm bubbling over. "People need to know about the positive change happening here. Your story could inspire others to create similar spaces. How about we sit down for an interview later today?"

Surprise and gratitude swirled within Emma as she processed the editor's words. "Thank you for considering us for your article," she replied sincerely, her hazel eyes bright with emotion. "Let's do it. I'd be honored to share our story with the community."

Emma and the editor sat in a quiet corner of the café, the gentle hum of conversation and the aroma of freshly brewed coffee enveloping them. The editor adjusted their recorder and leaned attentively as Emma began to speak.

"You see," Emma started, her voice infused with passion, "Serendipity Café wasn't always like this. When I first started working here, it was just another coffee shop. But I always believed in the power of small gestures to make a big difference."

She glanced around the bustling café, where patrons engaged in lively discussions or enjoyed moments of quiet reflection. "I began leaving little notes—words of encouragement and kindness—around the café. It was a simple idea, but the response was overwhelming. People started noticing, and those notes sparked conversations and connections."

The editor nodded, scribbling notes as Emma spoke. "The transformation wasn't just about physical space," Emma continued. "It was about creating a welcoming environment where everyone feels seen and heard. A place where struggles are shared and celebrated, and where each person who walks through that door knows they matter."

The editor looked up, their eyes reflecting Emma's passion. "It's incredible," they commented. "And how do you envision this impacting other businesses in town?"

Emma smiled thoughtfully. "I hope our story inspires others," she replied earnestly. "Not just cafés or restaurants, but all businesses. Imagine if every shop and office became a place where people felt valued and understood. It would create a ripple effect of positivity and community across our town."

The editor nodded. "Absolutely," they said, tapping their pen against the notepad. "Your vision is powerful, Emma. I think our readers will be inspired by what you've created here."

As the interview concluded, Emma felt a deep sense of satisfaction. Sharing Serendipity Café's journey with a broader audience was more than just publicity—it was an opportunity to ignite change and spread hope. She watched as the editor gathered their belongings, knowing that together, they would share a story that could touch hearts and inspire kindness far beyond the cozy walls of the café.

Amidst the ongoing celebration at Serendipity Café and the heartfelt echoes of stories shared, a new chapter began to unfold—the narrative of Emma's journey and the café's profound role as a sanctuary of kindness, poised to extend its influence beyond its familiar confines. The unexpected visit from the local newspaper editor had marked a turning point, promising to amplify the café's message of community, warmth, and genuine connection.

In the following days, Emma leaned over the counter and looked around the room. She reflected on the journey that had led her to this moment. A journey of small gestures and heartfelt notes that had transformed a simple café. She envisioned the article inspiring others in the community, to foster similar havens of compassion where every individual could find a connection.

The Art of Forgiveness

Bella and James, two childhood friends, were bound by an almost magical connection. From the moment they could walk, they were side by side, drifting through the streets of their small town. They navigated their early years together, exploring enchanted forests conjured by their vivid imaginations and embarking on daring adventures that only they could see. Their loyalty to one another was unwavering, a silent vow that needed no words. The townsfolk often paused to watch them, two kindred spirits whose bond was as inspiring as it was unbreakable.

Through sun-drenched summers and snow-blanket winters, Bella and James faced the world. Each day was a new chapter in their unfolding story, filled with the kind of pure, unfiltered joy that seemed to elude so many. Bella and James were more than just friends; they were the heart and soul of each other's lives, their shared history a treasure trove of cherished memories and unspoken promises.

From skipping stones across the tranquil pond to sketching fantastical worlds in the margins of their schoolbooks, Bella and James were kindred spirits. Their friendship was secret and understanding. They admired each other deeply, and their futures seemed intertwined in the most innocent ways.

They wove their childhood tales like expert storytellers in the embrace of sun-soaked afternoons. Laughter echoed through the fields as they skipped stones across the shimmering pond. Bella and James weren't just friends. They were adventurers in a world of their own making, where every corner of their small town held the promise of discovery.

One summer, they transformed the old, abandoned barn at the edge of town into a pirate ship. Armed with wooden swords and makeshift eye patches, they became Captain Bella and First Mate James, sailing the high seas in search of hidden treasure. They crafted intricate maps and braved imaginary storms, their shouts of triumph and daring resonating through the dusty rafters. Once a forgotten relic, the barn became a fortress, its wooden beams echoing with the spirit of their adventures.

In the spring, they turned the meadow behind Bella's house into an enchanted forest. With flower crowns adorning their heads and capes billowing behind them, they ventured into a realm where fairies danced in the moonlight, and ancient trees whispered secrets. They created elaborate stories of noble quests and magical creatures, their imaginations painting the landscape with vibrant hues of wonder.

The meadow, awash in the fragrance of wildflowers, became their sanctuary, where reality and fantasy intertwined in a seamless dance.

During the crisp autumn months, the pair became intrepid explorers, mapping out every inch of the town's surrounding woods. They crafted leaf-covered journals filled with sketches of mythical beasts and detailed descriptions of their adventures. Each discovery, whether an unusually shaped rock or a hidden grove, was a cause for celebration and a new entry in their ever-growing anthology of tales.

When snow blanketed the ground in winter, they became arctic explorers navigating the tundra. The world outside their windows transformed into a landscape of glistening white, perfect for building igloos and staging epic snowball battles. Their cheeks flushed with cold and excitement. They declared themselves guardians of the snow kingdom, defending it from the imaginary invaders that lurked just beyond the tree line.

These adventures weren't just fleeting moments of play. They were the threads that wove together their friendship. Bella and James stitched their dreams and boundless imagination into every story, creating a rich, shared history that would outlast even the most vivid of their childhood fantasies. Through each season, their bond grew more robust, their shared adventures enduring the power of friendship and the limitless possibilities of the imagination.

Their youthful hearts danced in sync, fueled by a relentless curiosity that painted their world with hues of wonder and possibility. With every brush stroke on a canvas or every pencil scratch on paper, they found a common language through which their feelings flowed, unburdened by words.

In the quietude of their moments, glances were exchanged, and a knowing look held reassurance in moments of uncertainty and laughter in sheer delight. Their connection transcended the mere articulation of thoughts; it was a dialogue resonating in the gentle rustle of leaves and the melodious chirping of birds.

Amidst the chaos of their youthful adventures, they stood as allies, supporting each other through the tempests and triumphs of life. Each climbed up a tree to uncover hidden hideouts or explore the dense woods.

Their world is painted with vivid passions, a masterpiece crafted by their intertwined souls. The mere sight of Bella's infectious smile or James' twinkling eyes held within them an entire universe.

Underneath the sprawling oak tree, Bella and James sat cross-legged, their sketchbooks sprawled open, capturing the essence of the world around them. The rustling leaves provided a soothing backdrop as they dipped their brushes into vibrant hues, painting landscapes existing in their imagination.

Her eyes wide with wonder, Bella pointed to the fluffy clouds drifting across the azure sky. "Look, James! Doesn't one resemble a soaring dragon?"

James grinned, his charcoal pencil darting across the page to capture the cloud's shape. "Over there," he exclaimed, pointing, "is the castle where the dragon resides!"

Laughter intertwined with the whispers of the wind as they wove stories of mythical creatures and epic quests. Imaginations crafted worlds that danced between reality and fantasy.

On another sunny afternoon, they perched on the edge of the wooden dock, feet skimming the crystalline surface of the pond. Bella skipped a stone across the water, creating ripples painted a mosaic of reflections.

"Bella," James began, gazing at the rippling water, "each ripple tells a story, just like the strokes on our canvases."

Bella nodded, her eyes sparkling. "It's like our friendship—every moment, every adventure, leaving a mark lasts forever."

In the quiet hours of twilight, they sought refuge in the attic of Bella's house, surrounded by forgotten treasures and relics of the past. Dust danced in the golden rays filtering through the attic window as they rummaged through old trinkets. "Remember when we thought your grandma's ancient vase cursed?" she chuckled, a mischievous glint in her eye, as James grinned, recalling their comical misadventures." She held up a worn-out paintbrush, a relic from their childhood escapades. "Remember this? It's the brush we used to paint our grand masterpiece—the secret garden!"

James chuckled. "Yes! We turned a corner of the garden into a magical realm. Those were the days, Bella."

The attic was a treasure trove of memories, with old books stacked haphazardly, creaking floorboards beneath their feet, and childhood relics scattered everywhere. As they sifted through dusty photo albums and tried on forgotten costumes, their conversation about the simplest things turned into a symphony of laughter and shared stories, reflecting the strength of their promising friendship.

Bella and James navigated the web of adolescence, their once unbreakable bond tested by the tumultuous currents of change. The sights and sounds of their world transformed, mirroring the evolution of their friendship.

Their laughter, echoing through sun-dappled meadows, now conveyed uncertainty amidst the bustling hallways in the high school corridors. Hesitant pauses and guarded words now punctuated conversations flowed.

In the ebb and flow of their teenage years, new interests emerged, sculpting their worlds in divergent shapes. Bella found comfort in the quiet sanctuary of art studios, her canvases a refuge where emotions were expressed in vivid strokes. James sought support in the whirlwind of sports fields and academic pursuits, his ambitions driving him toward uncharted territories.

A glance exchanged in the crowded hallways, a fleeting smile in passing, carried within them the remnants of a bond time and distance couldn't erase. Their relationship shifted, like tectonic plates reshaping the earth's surface, creating new contours and landscapes. Bella and James went through the ups and downs of adolescence, changing schools, making new friends, and discovering their individual passions. Despite these changes, their friendship remained steadfast and true.

It began with a careless whisper that spiraled into a storm. In a moment of unintended indiscretion, Bella had mentioned James' family troubles to a classmate. "It's been tough for James," she had said, not realizing the weight of her words. "His parents are getting divorced."

James found out on a chilly autumn afternoon, the air crisp with the scent of fallen leaves. He approached Bella, his face flushed with hurt and anger. "Why did you tell them?" His voice trembled with a raw edge that Bella had never heard before.

She blinked, taken aback. "James, I didn't mean—"

"I heard what I heard, Bella!" He cut her off, eyes blazing. "Why did you do that?" His words, sharp and accusing, pierced the fragile bubble of their friendship.

Bella's heart sank. She reached out a hand, but James stepped back, his expression a mix of betrayal and pain. "I thought you understood," he said, quieter now but no less wounded. "I trusted you."

"I didn't mean to hurt you," Bella pleaded, her voice barely above a whisper. "I was just..."

"Just what? Sharing my secrets?" James shook his head, the distance between them growing with each word. "I can't believe you, Bella."

Bella's eyes were wide with urgency as she tried to explain, her voice tinged with regret. "James, please listen. It's not what you think. I didn't mean to hurt you." She reached out, her hand trembling slightly, but James stepped back, his jaw clenched and eyes flashing with hurt. The air was thick with unspoken words and misunderstandings. Bella's breath quickened as she desperately tried to bridge the growing chasm, her heart aching at the sight of James's pained expression.

Tension grew, and the courtyard felt tight and tense around them. Bella's eyes filled with tears as she begged for understanding, her voice shaking, "You didn't let me explain. Please, James, trust me."

James struggled with feeling disappointed and betrayed, his heart heavy. He expressed his pain quietly, saying, "I trusted you, Bella. I trusted you completely."

Their once familiar spaces felt foreign as if their world was unraveling. Bella's eyes, brimming with unshed tears, showed hurt and disbelief. His voice, tinged with frustration and anguish, struggled to express emotions just out of reach. Miscommunications tangled their friendship in unresolved feelings.

Bella and James felt the weight of their fractured friendship, casting a shadow over their lives. It carried an invisible burden, echoing remnants of their past conversations and leaving vacant spaces in their hearts.

Bella's loss of James was a constant ache, a void refusing to be filled. The sights that brought her joy were now dull, devoid of the vibrant hues James had painted into her world. The art studio now witnessed the absence, its canvases holding echoes of their dreams turned bitter.

James, too, carried the weight of their fractured bond like an anchor, dragging him through the currents of regret and longing. The sounds used to serenade his days—the laughter reverberating through the school corridors were distant, lost in the haunting silence of their misunderstanding.

The emotional toll of their separation lingered in the air, palpable in the apologies that remained lodged in their throats. It was an ache, a wound that refused to heal, as the memories of their shattered friendship whispered haunting echoes through their minds.

The sight of Bella's hesitant smile or James' wistful gaze bore witness to the void taken root between them, forged from misunderstandings and unspoken truths.

Their friendship became a gaping chasm, keeping them apart despite their yearning for reconciliation. Regrets, unresolved emotions, and deafening silence kept them shackled to the pain of their fractured bond, unable to bridge the gap time etched between them.

Time unfurled its relentless march, and James and Bella drifted apart. Footsteps echo in opposite directions yet are tethered by the lingering threads of their past. The emotional undertow of their fractured bond keeps their gazes fixed on the rearview mirror of their memories, even as they trudged forward into uncharted futures.

The sights which once bore the imprint of their friendship now showcased the stark contrast of their separate journeys. Bella's solitary figure, her silhouette painting poignant portraits in the art studio's twilight, echoed with the whispers of unfinished conversations. The sound of her brush against the canvas carried the weight of untold stories. A longing and nostalgia reverberated through the room.

James' footsteps echoed across bustling hallways, each stride carving a path toward unfamiliar destinations. The sounds accompanying his solitary walks were bustling crowds, laughter was distant, and the echoes of apologies underscored the absence of a once cherished presence.

Nevertheless, despite their separate orbits, the emotional gravity of their past remained an invisible tether, a beacon in the labyrinth of their divergent paths. Each carried the weight of unspoken words, a burden shaping their choices and coloring the tapestries of their lives.

The separation was a chasm that widened, but failed to sever the invisible thread binding their souls. They were on a journey toward separate horizons, yet both held to the fragments of their history, unable to completely relinquish the memories weaving them together.

They traversed their paths, the sights and sounds of their lives held echoes of a past they couldn't entirely leave behind. It was an emotional landscape painted with hues of longing, regret, and unwavering hope. Their paths might converge again someday amidst their divergent lives.

Bella's journey as a painter was an unwavering dedication and passion for the arts. In the wake of the fracture in her friendship with James, she sought console in the comforting embrace of paint and canvas. The art studio became her haven, a sanctuary of dreams, a cocoon where emotions flowed onto the waiting canvas.

She immersed herself in the art world, becoming an attentive student of the craft. Guided by mentors who recognized her raw talent and unyielding determination, Bella honed her skills, experimenting with brushstrokes that mirrored her moods. Each stroke became a narrative—a fusion of colors depicted her heart.

Her art conveyed tales of longing, resilience, and the yearning for reconciliation. Exhibitions showcased her soulful creations, each piece a window into her inner world, a world mirroring both the pain of the past and hope for the future.

In contrast, James, while pursuing a career in graphic design, found an unexpected solace in the quiet corners of his life. He wielded a paintbrush with a familiarity echoing their past. Despite the demands of his profession, the call of the canvas remained an unwavering presence, a companion in the chaos of his days.

James noticed himself drawn to the painting's colors and textures, creating artwork that echoed the untamed landscapes of his emotions. His creations held the essence of his heart. They were a tribute to his cherished bond and a homage to his friend.

His path as a graphic designer intertwined with moments stolen with a paintbrush, to their passion for art's indelible mark on his soul. His career led him down one road. His heart encountered comfort in the brushstrokes echoing their past.

Bella and James discovered their respective artistic pursuits on their distinct paths. Their paintbrushes became extensions of their souls, echoing the emotional landscapes of their journey—two separate narratives converging in the universal language of art.

James often grappled with the weight of unresolved emotions in the quiet moments of his solitary nights. His thoughts circled back to Bella like a moth drawn to a flickering flame. The familiarity of her number on his phone beckoned to him, an invitation to bridge the chasm separating them for so long.

He'd dial her number, his heart pounding with the weight of words and unsaid apologies. The phone would ring, each tone echoing like a drumbeat, the sound a cacophony of longing and uncertainty. The dial tone persisted. Uncertainty gripped him, paralyzing his tongue and forcing him to hang up—each aborted call left a lingering ache in his chest.

His mind was a whirlwind of conflicting feelings. The right words eluded him, drifting like elusive ghosts through the corridors of his thoughts. He yearned for a bridge to traverse the distance between them, but the fear of exacerbating the pain held him back.

James was at an impasse—a soul torn between the desire for reconciliation and the fear of inflicting further hurt. He was adrift in a sea of unresolved emotions, his longing for peace with his childhood confidante echoing through the nights.

The weight of their history pressed upon him, leaving him grappling with the enormity of their past. The unsent messages and unanswered calls stood as the chasm still lingered. A gap he yearned to bridge, but the words remained elusive.

Bella's paintings became a sanctuary where she wove her pain into strokes of vibrant hues and intricate patterns. With each brushstroke, she masked the raw edges of her emotions, using the canvas as a cathartic release for the turmoil within.

Themes emerged from the depths of her anguish, intermingling with the strokes of her brush. The pain fracturing her friendship with James became the muse for her art, infusing each creation with a haunting beauty born from her sorrow.

The depths of her heart spilled onto the canvas. They manifested in the contrasts of light and dark, the interplay of colors echoed the complexities of her heart. Scenes of fractured landscapes and isolated figures emerged with each stroke, an emotional terrain she traversed.

Her paintings became a language—a conversation with her soul. The artistry veiled the pain, allowing her to navigate the labyrinth of her feelings while creating a visual narrative echoing the ache she carried within.

Despite the mask her art provided, she found inspiration in these themes of pain. The tumultuous currents of her fractured friendship with James fueled her creative fire. It propelled her to explore the depths of emotion and infuse her art with raw, poignant honesty.

Each painting reflected the inner turmoil she grappled with, a canvas mirrored the journey toward healing—a journey intertwined with the pain that fueled her artistic expression.

The unexpected arrival of invitations to their hometown's art gallery honoring local talents startled both Bella and James. The envelopes held a surprise, stirring a whirlwind of emotions, catching them off guard, and setting their hearts racing.

The surprise invitations acted as unexpected messengers, reviving dormant sentiments and resurrecting fragments of their history. They left both Bella and James contemplating the possibility of revisiting a past they thought they had left behind, making the prospect of a reunion thrilling and uncertain.

In the quiet solitude of her thoughts, Bella grappled with the echoes of her past. A dialogue lingered in the recesses of her mind. The notion of returning home, an idea flickering like a distant beacon, gained momentum, its pull growing stronger with each passing day.

Her heart, an orchestra of conflicting moods, echoed the tumultuous landscapes of her past. Thoughts of James—the childhood friend she parted ways with—wove through her consciousness like a fragile thread, both painful and hopeful.

Amidst the quietude of her days, Bella's mind echoed with self-assurances the whispered promises she made to herself. "Perhaps it's time," she mused, the idea taking root in her heart. "Time to confront the echoes of our fractured bond."

Her hometown beckoned and drew her back to where their friendship had once bloomed. The catalyst prompting her return was a subtle convergence of circumstances. A chance encounter with an old photograph rekindled memories she had long tucked away. The image of her and James, laughter etched on their youthful faces, stirred a wave of longing and introspection, propelling her toward the inevitability of homecoming.

With a bittersweet mixture of apprehension and hope, Bella decided to return. The yearning for closure and the possibility of reconciliation cast a tentative ray of light into the shadows of their fractured bond. Emotions swirled within her—a whirlwind of nostalgia, trepidation, and an unwavering determination to confront the unresolved chapters of their history.

James held the invitation, and a rush of conflicting sensations surged. "Bella... hometown... unexpected," he murmured, sounding almost foreign to his ears. His furrowed brow betrayed the subtle turmoil churning beneath his composed facade. "What does this mean?" he mused aloud. Uncertainty filled his mind. Scenes of their past flashes filled his head of the last time that he saw her. The way they ended was not how he wanted it.

Nervous energy crackled at the edges of his being, and his chest tightened subtly as he imagined the implications of the invitation. The mention of Bella's name amidst the gallery details set off a whirlwind of feelings, a tempest brewing within him.

Like a whisper, a sense of apprehension lingered beneath the surface. The idea of revisiting their history, the potential of encountering Bella after years of separation. It left him both captivated and unnerved by the unexpected turn of events—a clandestine invitation seemed poised to reopen chapters long thought closed.

They roamed the corridors of the exhibition, a familiar piece caught Bella's eye—a painting echoing the emotional landscapes of their past.

Across the room, James, captivated by a display, held the essence of his artistic journey—a piece that resonated with the hues of his untold stories.

Interrupted by the interest that defined their bond, their paths led them closer, almost as if guided by an unseen force. Amidst the throng of art enthusiasts, their steps moved synchronously, drawing them closer to an unexpected intersection.

Bella and James found themselves standing in the heart of their hometown, surrounded by the familiar sights that once bore witness to their adventures. Their eyes met across the bustling streets, a brief pause in the rhythm of life as recognition dawned upon them. Bella's hesitant smile reflected his cautious gaze, carrying the weight of unspoken words and the echoes of their strained bond. As he extended his hand for a handshake,

caught up in the moment, Bella moved in for a friendly hug. James hesitated, arms awkwardly hovering in the air before he slowly reciprocated. For a brief, awkward second, their bodies were stiff, unsure how to navigate the sudden intimacy. Then, as their eyes met, absurdity hit them both. Laughter bubbled up, breaking the tension and filling the room with a joyful sound. They pulled back, still chuckling, the awkwardness dissolving into a hilariously sweet moment that reaffirmed their bond.

The silence between them grew heavy, stretching out until it felt like the world had paused. Bella's eyes searched James' face, desperate for a flicker of understanding, but all she saw was the rigid set of his jaw and the pain in his eyes.

A breeze rustled the leaves around them, but neither moved, locked in a wordless standoff. Bella's throat tightened as she watched James' hand clench into a fist and slowly release, the gesture betraying his inner turmoil. Her fingers itched to reach out, to bridge the hole that had suddenly stretched between them.

James' gaze wavered, flickering to the ground before lifting to meet Bella's again. She saw the ache of betrayal and a flicker of something else in his eyes—maybe a glimmer of hope that this wasn't the end. Bella's lips parted as if to speak, but the words wouldn't come, caught in the tangle of her regret.

A tear escaped her cheek, and she quickly brushed it away, hoping he hadn't noticed. But James had seen it, and his stern expression softened momentarily, a mirror of the turmoil that swirled within her. The air between them crackled with unspoken words, a fragile bridge of longing and remorse.

Finally, Bella took a tentative step forward, her heart pounding. She opened her mouth, trembling, and whispered, "James, please..."

James hesitated, his eyes locked on hers. The distance between them felt insurmountable, yet the unspoken conversation that passed in the silence held a tentative promise—that maybe, just maybe, there was still a chance to mend what was broken.

A familiar voice broke the trance, their mutual acquaintance a bridge ushering them toward a quiet corner, away from the bustling crowds. It was a sanctuary amidst the chaos, where conversations could finally find their voice.

Bella's voice quivered as she said, "It's been a while." Her words held layers of feelings—hesitation, longing, and a faint glimmer of hope.

He nodded in response, his gaze softening, "It has... too long." His voice held traces of regret.

The conversation unfolded like an orchestrated dance, a delicate balance of explanations and hesitant apologies. James fumbled with his words, creating a rather amusing mix-up of phrases. Bella couldn't help but stifle a laugh, breaking the tension. The laughter was a much-needed relief from the lingering awkwardness. They navigated the minefield of misunderstandings driving them apart, unraveling the knots of their fractured friendship with each chosen word.

Bella and James, amidst their conversation about their past, reminisced about the old art studio nestled in the basement of the studio. The dialogue kindled a spark of curiosity—a desire to revisit the space where their childhood creativity blossomed. \

They ventured to the stairs. It beckoned them, its steps creaking under the weight of their anticipation. They descended into the lit basement. The air thickened with the scent of old books and faint hints of dried paint. The fragrances evoked the essence of their history. Sunlight filtered through small windows, glowing on the room's corners.

Footsteps echoed against the concrete floor, an orchestra of memories resurfacing with each movement. The sight of dusty canvases leaning against the walls and forgotten art supplies stirred emotions that lay dormant within them.

Bella's voice, filled with wonder, broke the silence, "Here it is, our old studio!" Her words echoed a bygone era when the room had been a sanctuary for their artistic endeavors.

James nodded in agreement, a nostalgic smile playing on his lips. "This place holds a world of memories," he remarked, his gaze drifting to the familiar clutter that adorned the room.

Bella's voice trembled as she broke the silence, "The memories here are vivid."

James nodded, a nostalgic smile playing on his lips. "The laughter echoes through these walls," he replied, his gaze drifting to the faded sketches adorning the studio.

The ambiance held an air of familiarity and uncertainty—a mix of emotions painted on the canvas of their expressions. The sunlight filtered through dusty windows, glowing upon the worn easels and scattered paintbrushes.

A hint of hesitation lingered in their exchanged glances, a conversation echoing the desire for reconciliation. The subtle creaks of the old floorboards bore witness to the weight of their words.

Bella's fingers brushed the edge of an unfinished painting, tracing the outline of forgotten dreams. "We were once kindred spirits here," she murmured, her voice carrying an ache.

James reached for a nearby canvas, fingers tracing the brushstrokes left by his younger self. "The art spoke for us when words failed," he remarked, longing to lace his words.

In this space of artistic reminiscence, the air hummed with the possibility of rekindling what time and misunderstandings had frayed. Uncovering a rather amusing doodle of a whimsical creature, Bella chuckled, "Ah, the days when we thought these were our artistic triumphs."

Spotting an exaggerated landscape sketch, James joined in, "I'm sure the art world trembled at the sight of our masterpieces!"

Bella traced her finger along the edge of a dusty canvas in the quiet of the art studio, breaking the uneasy silence. "Remember how we splashed paint around and laughed for hours?" Her voice carried a hint of nostalgia, the words echoing the memories they once held dear.

James nodded, his gaze fixed on a half-finished sketch nearby. "Those were simpler times," he replied, the weight of their estrangement palpable in his tone. The room, adorned with remnants of their artistic escapades, stood as a witness to the echoes of their fractured friendship.

A hesitant pause lingered between them, the tensions crackling like static electricity. The memories of their falling out loomed large, an invisible barrier hindering the ease of their interaction. Each word spoken skirted the edges of deeper conversations they both longed to have.

The atmosphere held a subdued energy, the air thick with the scent of dried paint and the faint rustling of papers. Once a haven of creativity, the studio was heavy with unresolved passions—a poignant reminder of the rift driving them apart.

The art studio, a sanctuary of forgotten creativity, brimmed with canvases stacked against the walls and shelves cluttered with paints and brushes. Bella and James, both skilled artists, found solace in the familiar sight of their tools—an invitation to express what words failed to convey.

She hesitated before picking up a brush, her gaze fixed on the blank canvas. "I used to find my voice through painting," she remarked, carrying a tinge of vulnerability and longing.

His eyes focused on a palette of vibrant colors, nodded in understanding. "Sometimes, the canvas speaks louder than words," he replied, a faint trace of remorse coloring his words.

The sound of brushstrokes against canvas filled the air, a gentle rhythm punctuating the quietude of the studio. She couldn't resist a grin, nudging him and quipping, 'I think my dog paints better!' The lighthearted banter wove into their artistic pursuits, adding a touch of levity to the room. Each stroke echoed the feelings swirling within—the weight of remorse, the ache of lost companionship, and the tentative hope for reconciliation.

During the artistic fervor, James, with a mischievous grin, quipped, "Well, I hope the art world is ready for our unparalleled genius." Followed by a huge laughter, prompting laughter.

Colors mingled on the canvases. Their paintings became a dialogue—a language they both understood. The atmosphere buzzed with a blend of emotions, the room alive with the raw expression of their feelings and the yearning for closure. Bella stumbled upon a dusty sketch from their teenage years, depicting an exaggerated scene.

Each brushstroke transformed into a conversation—a profound expression of sentiments. Trembling with the weight of unexpressed longing, Bella dipped the brush into the palette, selecting hues mirroring the depths of her turmoil. Swirls of paint cascaded onto the canvas, each stroke a whispered lamentation, echoing the ache of a fractured bond.

Her hand moved with a mix of trepidation and urgency, the rhythm of her strokes capturing the fragments of regret lingering in the air. Colors mingled, interlacing the complexities of her heart. Blues bled into grays, conveying the melancholy clinging to her memories' edges. Each brushstroke etched a tale of missed conversations and an unyielding desire for reconciliation.

The colors met the blank space. His strokes painted a mosaic of sentiments. Swirls of crimson, representing the anger of misunderstanding, juxtaposed against streaks of gold. It whispered of cherished moments now lost in the labyrinth of time. The creation bore witness to his regrets and longing, and the words weighed on his soul.

The atmosphere hummed with emotions with every dab of paint. The rhythmic tap of brushes against the canvas and the faint scent of drying paint mingled with the palpable tension in the air. Each stroke unraveled a fragment of their past, the clashing hues and gentle blends as a tumultuous journey.

The artwork spoke where conversations faltered, capturing the ache of separation and the yearning for closure. An exchange of colors unfolded, each hue carrying its apology. The echoes of laughter, now lost to time, lingered in the air, mingling with the longing for a rekindled bond. Together, these elements saturated the studio with an emotional resonance transcending mere words.

They found themselves side by side, their brushes dancing across the canvas in a duet. The artistic styles merged with each stroke, weaving their fractured friendship's tentative reconnection.

Laden with hues of melancholy and longing, Bella's brush is now intertwined with his vibrant strokes, each movement a bridge between their divergent emotions. The bold strokes she employed softened, melding seamlessly with his vivid palette, creating a kaleidoscope of feelings on the canvas.

They painted together, and a harmonious synergy emerged. Bella's gentle curves and subtle gradients intertwined with his bold lines and vibrant splashes. The merging of their distinct styles echoed the gradual reconciliation of their once estranged bond—a symbolic dance of sentiments and healing.

Amidst their collaborative efforts, their conversation floated like a rhythmic brush meeting canvas.

"Your strokes are lively today," Bella commented, her brush moving.

He focused on the canvas and replied, "Trying to infuse some energy. It's been lacking."

"Let me soften it a bit," Bella said, blending her colors seamlessly.

"Yeah, your touch might balance things out," James nodded, his attention still fixed on their evolving creation.

The dialogue intertwines with the visual narrative they were crafting, each word and stroke contributing to the evolving harmony of their artwork.

The atmosphere hummed with the rhythmic sound of brushes meeting canvas, creating apologies and tentative hope. Heavy with unresolved emotions, the studio vibrated with the energy of their collaborative effort and conversation, like a live wire crackling with electric anticipation.

Their movements synchronized, each stroke becoming a conversation. The studio witnessed a beautiful collision of contrasting colors and harmonious blends—a visual representation of their journey toward understanding and forgiveness.

With every brushstroke, the emotional depth of their canvas deepened. The sight of Bella's gentle strokes merging seamlessly with James' bold flourishes found tentative harmony in their artistic expression. Side by side, their brushes became extensions of thoughts and feelings, weaving a narrative transcending verbal expression.

The disparate artistic styles blended with each stroke into a seamless dance of colors and forms. Bella's once-subdued strokes harmonized with his bold flourishes that spoke volumes about their experiences.

They painted without speaking, yet their exchange was vibrant and poignant. Their brushes' gentle sways and purposeful movements conveyed the ebb and flow of regret, longing, and tentative hope.

The air crackled with creative energy as their understanding deepened. The sounds of their brushes sweeping across the canvas echoed a conversation, a language born from the fusion of their artistic expressions.

Bella's delicate strokes were interwoven with James' daring lines, forming a visual narrative of their evolving connection. The fusion of their once-disparate styles became a visual metaphor for the understanding and empathy blooming between them.

In this act of creation, the studio walls bore witness to a language beyond words. Each stroke was a declaration of empathy, a bridge between their past differences. The canvas transformed under their joint efforts, and a deeper understanding grew, surpassing the limitations of spoken language.

They delved into their creation, and Bella and James unraveled the tangled knots of their past. Amid the dance of colors on the canvas, the weight of words lifted, and they began to bridge the chasm separating them.

Bella's tentative voice sliced through the air, breaking the silence of their artistic communion. "Remember that day at the gallery?" Her brush paused, the bristles leaving a soft imprint on the canvas.

James nodded, his gaze fixed on the intertwining strokes. "I misunderstood. I thought..." His voice trailed off, the words echoing in the studio.

Dialogue unfurled in hues and shapes, each stroke a precursor to a confession or a revelation. Their perspectives clarified misunderstandings that had festered for years.

"I didn't mean to undermine your work," James confessed, his strokes faltering. "I was so lost in my insecurities."

Bella's response was a gentle stroke, a blend of understanding and acknowledgment. "I felt dismissed, but I understand it now."

The studio walls absorbed their words and emotions, becoming witnesses to a cathartic exchange. Pauses and intakes of breath punctuated the rhythmic sound of brushes against the canvas, each moment a step towards reconciliation.

They continued painting, and their voices gained momentum, weaving a narrative pieced together fragments of misunderstandings and regrets. The sight of their synchronized movements and the rise and fall of their voices echoed the gradual unburdening of their hearts.

Through their creation, they found a safe space to express their vulnerabilities. The colors on the canvas reflected their journey—of acknowledging mistakes, seeking and giving forgiveness, and tentative steps toward rebuilding what had been fractured.

Each stroke of their brushes echoed their story, painting a picture of redemption and forgiveness in vibrant hues. The atmosphere in the studio crackled with tension, yet also with the promise of resolution. They painted, their conversation deepened, touching the raw nerves of past wounds and unraveling the knots of resentment and pain accumulated over time.

Their voices, now softer yet resonant with emotion, wove through the air, carrying the weight of their apologies and newfound understanding. "I understand now how my actions hurt you," James murmured, his brush moving in graceful arcs across the canvas.

Bella's response was a blend of empathy and release. "I held onto the hurt for so long. I'm ready to let it go." Her strokes danced alongside his, creating a harmony of colors and emotions.

The brushes became an extension of their reconciling spirits. With each stroke, forgiveness flowed, washing away the layers of bitterness and misunderstanding clouding their friendship.

Bella and James faced each other, their previous tensions now a backdrop to their creative collaboration. Their brushes moved with a renewed tracing of vivid lines and bold colors across the canvas. The once chaotic splatters of paint gradually blended into a harmonious composition, each stroke mirroring their emotional journey. The canvas now teemed with a rich tapestry of hues and textures, embodying their unfolding forgiveness. The colors mingled and merged, capturing the essence of their mutual understanding and healing in a visual symphony of artistry and emotion.

The movements synchronized as they painted side by side, mirroring the newfound harmony in their hearts. The weight burdening them for so long dissipated, carried away by the rhythm of their collaborative creation.

During their artistic expression, a profound sense of liberation enveloped them. The studio resonated with a serene energy, the sounds of their brushes against the canvas transforming into reconciliation.

Bella and James stood amidst the transformed studio. Their final strokes marked the culmination of their journey—a masterpiece born not only of paint but of mutual understanding and absolution. They have an agreement—a vow to move forward, leaving behind the shadows of their fractured past. Emotion washed over them. Their eyes met, shimmering with unshed tears, conveying an understanding of words never captured.

"It's like a beginning," Bella whispered, her voice trembling with emotion.

He nodded, his throat tightening with a mix of relief and gratitude. "A fresh start."

Their breaths synchronized, and the weight of past grievances lifted from their shoulders, leaving a profound sense of liberation. The once-divided canvases now stood as evidence of their reconciliation, healing, and newfound understanding journey.

A single tear traced a path down Bella's cheek, reflecting the kaleidoscope of emotions swirling within her. He reached out, brushing it away. A wordless gesture spoke volumes.

The studio echoed with the fading of their laughter, a reconciliation resonating in the now-hallowed space. The sunlight streamed through the windows, casting a golden glow upon their transformed sanctuary.

"It's like coming home," James murmured, a sense of wonder lacing his words.

Bella nodded, her heart brimming with gratitude for this rekindled connection. "Home... yes, it does."

The embrace spoke of forgiveness and understanding, of the profound beauty of second chances. The past dissolved into insignificance, overshadowed by the promise of a future filled with laughter and renewed friendship.

Bella and James stepped outside, Lightened by the release of old burdens. The door closed behind them, marking the end of a chapter tainted with misunderstandings and pain and the beginning of a new, uncharted journey together.

They ventured into the world. The studio stood a witness—a sanctuary borne witness to the resurrection of a bond once thought lost. The sun dipped below the horizon, casting the sky in hues of orange and pink—a breathtaking metaphor for the beauty born from healing and forgiveness.

The Music of Healing

Clara moved with quiet grace, her eyes shining with fiery enthusiasm. She scanned the world around her, absorbing every detail as if each moment were a note waiting to be played. People passing by caught glimpses of her in flowing dresses, each movement mirroring the grace of her artistry.

She was a maestro of the violin. The stage was her universe. Her slender fingers haunted songs that danced through the air and cast a spell upon the audience. Like a thunderous ocean, the cadence of applause washed over her, amplifying the adrenaline thrummed beneath her skin.

The violin nestled against her neck. With each stroke of the bow, she channeled a torrent of sorrow and joy and craved into the strings of sound that painted landscapes of the heart. It wasn't a performance but a revelation, an unveiling of the rawest parts of her soul.

Offstage, her presence was a magnetism that drew admirers and curious onlookers alike. She revealed herself in the hushed moments backstage, where the performance still reverberated in her veins. She lived for moments on stage where her heart sang its most authentic song.

Clara was not only a performer but also a teacher. Her gaze, bright with enthusiasm, fell upon the eager faces of her young students, as she

guided students with patience and grace, and Clara nurtured a fervent devotion to it. Her melodious voice carried snippets of encouragement and guidance, steering tiny hands across the strings. She didn't dictate; she inspired and coaxed out the harmonies hidden in each child's heart.

The room brimmed with an orchestra of laughter, frustrated sighs, and triumphant exclamations when a difficult passage was mastered. Each lesson wasn't just a tutorial; it was a spellbinding enchantment, casting a magical aura over everyone present. She didn't just share techniques; she unveiled the soulful unification between artist and instrument. Her love flowed into her teaching, infusing the room and transcending the confines of the classroom.

Beyond the mechanics of playing the violin, Clara sought to unveil the magic—the ability of harmony to stir feelings, tell stories, and evoke memories. The children's faces lit up with understanding and joy. She wasn't just teaching them notes; she was igniting a lifelong affair with a song that would resonate in their souls long after the lesson ended.

On a moonlit night, the concert hall exuded an afterglow of applause as she exited the venue. The city's streets buzzed with life, the air infused with the aroma of street food and the distant hum of traffic. Settling into her car, she felt a sense of calm. But as she drove, the sound of screeching tires came closer, piercing the post-performance tranquility in her mind. An abrupt chaos unfolded as metal collided and glass shattered.

A cacophony of alarms blared, blending with the acrid odor of burnt rubber and the metallic tang of blood in the air. Clara's senses reeled, overwhelmed by the sudden chaos and devastation.

Amidst the blurred lights and the whirling chaos, Clara's body absorbed the impact. Pain tore through her, not just physical but a rending of the spirit, a sudden disconnection from her music. The violin, her companion and source of comfort, lay crushed amidst the wreckage.

Tears blurred her vision and mirrored the shattered pieces of her once-hopeful future. The night that held the promise of triumph now cradled the fragments of her musical identity and left her stranded in disbelief and loss.

In the blurred boundary between wakefulness and oblivion, Clara hovered, her consciousness drifting on the edge of silence. Amidst the haze, distant voices resonated—the urgent cadence of people in white coats and scrubs moving with purpose. Bright, sterile lights shone overhead, casting harsh shadows. Some wore masks and spoke rapidly, their conversations blending into a symphony of medical jargon.

The sharp scent of antiseptic filled the air, mingling with the faint aroma of latex and alcohol wipes. Machines beeped rhythmically, and the rustle of paper and fabric was added to the backdrop. Through the confusion, their words carried a sense of hope and urgency, a lifeline amidst the chaos.

In fleeting moments of consciousness, she experienced a desperate tug-of-war between her mind and the darkness that threatened to envelop her. The sensation of numbness fought against the twinges of pain.

Clara was suspended between dreams and reality. Her eyes fluttered open to the harsh fluorescence of the hospital room, and the faint aroma of disinfectant lingered.

Her gaze fell upon her hands. One hand, swathed in bandages, lay still, an immobilized sentinel. The other remained intact.

In the lonely confines of her room, she grappled with the weight of her altered reality. Once brimming with determination, her expression now mirrored a storm of sorrow and frustration. The lines of her face were etched deeply as if the weight of unspoken fears and dashed hopes had pressed down upon her. Her posture was tense, shoulders hunched as if bracing against an unseen tempest. The intensity of her emotions was evident, swirling within her like dark clouds gathering before a storm.

She reached for her violin case with trembling hands, the soft click of the latches seeming to echo her dread. When she opened it, the sight of her beloved violin, shattered and splintered, brought her to her knees. The fragments of wood and broken strings were a cruel reflection of her broken heart. The room fell into a heartrending silence, the weight of her loss sinking in as she clutched the remnants, tears streaming down her face.

She couldn't contain the surge of anguish any longer. With a primal scream, she let her fury rip through the suffocating silence that surrounded her. Her sobs followed, raw and unrestrained, as she collapsed to the floor, her cries echoing the depth of her shattered heart.

Every passing moment she witnessed was a crescendo of despair, an unyielding wave of feelings crashing against the shores of her shattered dreams. The lost opportunities mingled with the bitter flavor of resignation as Clara grappled with the stark reality of a future devoid of her music.

"Your hand won't regain its former dexterity," the words fell into the quiet space. The doctors, their voices measured and solemn, spoke in technical terms that painted a bleak picture. The sound of their prognosis struck a dissonant chord in Clara's mind and echoed the harshness of her new reality.

Her manager, usually vibrant with plans and positivity, approached with empathy and professional detachment. "Clara, we must consider the future," they began. The conversation, with vibrant visions, now navigated the daunting truth of an uncertain career. She noticed the sincerity in her manager's eyes. It was a stark contrast to the weight of the conversation. Each sentence shattered aspirations and unfulfilled ambitions.

Clara's voice trembled as she spoke to Dr. Reynolds. "I'm finding it so hard," Clara admitted. "Simple things... I can't seem to manage them anymore."

"It's a process. You're making progress, even slower than you'd like."

"It's infuriating!" Clara's frustration boiled over as she slammed her fist against the table, the force making the dishes clatter. She paced the room, her steps heavy and rapid, her fingers gripping her hair in exasperation. "I used to do these things. Now, it's an impossible task."

He reassured her, "The journey to recovery can be challenging, but we're here to support you through it."

She sank into the chair, her shoulders drooping as she stared at the floor. Her voice emerged as a soft, weary murmur, "I just want things to get better and find myself again."

"We understand," he affirmed. "It takes time, and it's normal. We're doing everything possible to help you regain your strength."

She nodded, her gratitude mingled with frustration. "Thank you. I'm trying. It's just hard to detect progress sometimes."

"Keep pushing forward. Even small victories pave the way to bigger ones. We're in this together."

"Thank you." Dr. Reynolds leaned forward.

"I understand this has been challenging," he handed her the brochure. "There's a clinic I recommend. It integrates music therapy into its physical and emotional healing approach."

Clara's brows furrowed, skepticism and a flicker of hope dancing in her eyes. "Music therapy?"

"Yes," he nodded. "They have innovative methods, incorporating rhythm and performance to aid improvement. It's shown remarkable results, especially in cases like yours."

Clara's hesitation hung on like an echo in the room. The idea was a departure from traditional therapy, and a glimmer of curiosity sparked within her. "How does that help... with everything?"

"It can have a profound impact, not just physiologically," he explained. "It engages different brain parts, aiding in motor skills, cognitive function, and emotional expression. It might offer a path forward, Clara."

She mulled over his words, the prospect seeming both daunting and appealing. After a moment's contemplation, she sighed. "Okay, I'll... consider it."

Dr. Reynolds smiled. "It's a step. I believe it might be significant. Let's explore this together."

Her fingers traced the edge of the brochure detailing the rehabilitation center's program.

Dr. Reynolds' words etched in her mind, his encouragement a flickering beacon amid her doubts. The prospect of reclaiming what had been taken from her danced tantalizingly at the edges of her thoughts.

In the following days, Clara's heart wrestled with the unfamiliarity of the idea. The brochure resting on her bedside table symbolized newfound hope. Clara sat tightly clasped in her lap, her fingers digging into her palms as her mind raced with swirling emotions. Her breath came in shallow, uneven bursts, reflecting a mixture of nervous anticipation and a fragile thread of hope. Her eyes flickered with a hesitant light whenever she thought about the possibility of finding happiness through therapy, mingling with the weight of her fears and doubts.

She folded the brochure into her pocket. This was a crucial step toward regaining what had been lost. Dr. Reynolds' hope became her own, an aspiration for a future intertwined with possibilities waiting to be rediscovered.

Clara arrived at the rehabilitation center. The facility stood nestled amidst serene surroundings, framed by lush greenery that soothed her nerves. The sight of the modern architecture, with its large windows inviting natural light, stood in stark contrast to the sterile hospital environment she'd grown accustomed to.

Her gaze swept across the entrance. The sound of laughter and gentle chatter drifted through the air, blending with the soft strains of a tune playing in the distance. It was a bustling life, a stark contrast to the clinical silence of the hospital corridors.

Emotions danced in Clara. The welcoming ambiance was a stark departure from her initial reservations. The tableau whispered promises of healing, a canvas painted with the hues of potential and possibility.

With each step into the facility, Clara's apprehension softened. The sight of individuals engaged in various activities—a group discussing music theory in one corner, others practicing instruments—inspired a spark of excitement. Clara's heart swelled with optimism as she embarked on this uncharted journey. It was a place where the language was ready to write a new chapter in her life.

A young woman greeted Clara. "Hi there, I'm Abby. I'll be showing you to your room," she said, her voice carrying a reassuring tone.

Clara sensed a wave of gratitude for Abby's welcoming demeanor, a smile curving her lips. "Nice to meet you, Abby. I'm Clara," she replied, her voice betraying a hint of relief.

Abby pointed out various areas as they walked—a communal lounge filled with cozy seating and instruments, a serene courtyard with benches and lush greenery, and the sounds of laughter and soft melodies infused the space with an inviting charm.

Clara's feelings were a combination of wonder and tentative hope, her heart stirred by the lively energy. It was a glimpse into a world brimming with vitality, where people pursued their paths to healing.

"Here's your room, Clara," said Abby. "Make yourself comfortable. If you need anything, ask."

Clara nodded with a warm smile. The room, though simple, exuded a sense of serenity. The soft light filtering through the window painted a tranquil ambiance. It was quiet where Clara hoped to rediscover the melodies that once filled her life.

With a reassuring smile, Abby assisted Clara in preparing dinner. She guided her through simple tasks, helping her select an outfit and arrange her belongings.

Clara's eyes wandered as they made their way to an available table. They took in the diverse assembly of individuals engaged in conversations, their hands punctuating their words with gestures. The sound of laughter intertwined with snippets of discussion filled the air.

Abby's presence beside her offered a sense of familiarity amid the unfamiliar. Clara found herself drawn into the rhythm of the bustling dining room, the sights and sounds of hope and belonging. It was a glimpse into a community united by shared aspirations of healing and renewal. A prospect that stirred a glimmer of optimism within Clara's heart.

Some faces were unfamiliar, while others bore expressions of recognition. A few whispered amongst themselves, recognizing Clara from her past performances on stage.

A flutter of unease danced in her chest as she received the recognition, her eyes shifting nervously while a small, satisfied smile tugged at the corners of her lips. The conflicting emotions played across her face, visible in the way her hands fidgeted, and her gaze darted around, trying to balance the discomfort with a touch of pleasure. The sights and sounds around her were vibrant interactions.

She settled into a seat. Conversations faded and flowed around her, personal stories, struggles, and the joy of newfound connections—the fragrant aromas of delectable dishes intertwined with the melodies of friendly banter, inclusivity, and warmth.

Despite her initial apprehension, she was drawn into this community of resilience and renewal. The recognition from those who remembered her performances tugged at the strings of her heart. It promised a rekindled love with her music and a newfound sense of belonging.

Among those who recognized Clara sat Alex, a mute pianist engrossed in a notebook. As their gazes met, Alex raised an eyebrow, a nonverbal greeting with a levity touch. She couldn't help but smile in response.

Clara was drawn to his subtle joking as the evening unfolded. Easing their initial tension. The sound of his light chuckles threaded through the din of conversations. Although he could not speak, he was very eager to listen. Each exchange, whether in the form of a written message or a gesture, depicted his unwavering love for music.

Clara's eyes widened as she opened Alex's notebook, revealing pages brimming with intricate sketches and musical notations. The delicate, looping lines of the drawings seemed to flow into the precise symbols and notes scattered across the pages, creating artistry and music. Each turn of the page offered a new glimpse into Alex's creative world, drawing Clara deeper into its fascinating complexity.

Clara appreciated his uplifting spirit. His humor was a gentle reminder that, despite their challenges, there was room for laughter and joy on their rehabilitation journey. This initial encounter set the tone for a friendship built on a mutual love for song and understanding. Both recognized that comedy may be an instrument in navigating the complexities of their healing paths.

Clara continued her journey at the rehabilitation center, and a sense of gradual improvement began to weave into her daily routines. The once-daunting tasks became more manageable, and she made remarkable strides in her rehabilitation.

Triumph surged through Clara, replacing the initial frustration and apprehension she had experienced. Each small victory— once challenging maneuvering tasks—sparked a newfound confidence.

Clara's progress was a crescendo of resilience. The sights, sounds, and scents around her painted a vivid picture of a community united by a common goal—a journey toward healing and renewed strength.

Clara's fingers danced over the strings of her unplayable violin, conjuring invisible melodies in the air. He was seated at the piano nearby and witnessed her movements, his hands mirroring the nuances of her imagined music on the keys.

With a soft smile, Clara glanced at him and wrote in her notebook, "Thank you for playing along." She showed the words to Alex, who responded with a nod and a warm smile, scribbling a quick note in his book.

"Your composition speaks," read Clara's note

Alex wrote back. "Your melodies inspire."

Their written exchange continued silently in the corner of the rehabilitation center. Their conversations became a refuge for their deepest narratives in their burgeoning companionship. Their bond grew as she revealed the emotional wreckage left by her accident. He, in turn, conveyed the trauma that rendered him mute. The quiet room, draped in warm hues of sunlight, witnessed their exchanges where empathy flowed, embracing quiet confessions.

Abby stood by as Clara exercised. Her eyes sparkled with excitement, her hands gesturing animatedly. She described how. Her fingers would glide over the violin strings. When she talked about Alex, a warm smile spread across her face, and she recounted their shared moments with a sense of joy and affection, evident in how she leaned forward and her enthusiasm. She told her about her rediscovered love for music and her friendship with Alex. "I never thought I'd feel that rush again," she expressed, her eyes alight.

Abby listened. "It's incredible how it has that effect, isn't it?"

She flexed her fingers around the exercise ball, recalling their profound encounters. "It's like our instruments spoke for us," she said, smiling. "Even without words, we found a way to communicate through melodies."

Abby's curiosity sparked. "It must've been a unique form of connection," she mused.

She nodded, the memory vivid in her mind. "It's like our love for it bridged the gap between us. We exchanged ideas, feelings—all without saying a word," she explained, the nostalgia evident in her tone.

The room felt charged, and her animated gestures punctuated the air as she recounted her experiences. Their conversation's sounds intertwined with the therapeutic exercises' background rhythm.

As they conversed, Abby witnessed the emotional depth behind Clara's words—the joy of rediscovery and the profound connection she found through music. Her eyes shimmered, stirred by her journey, and her gestures conveyed the intricacies of her bond with Alex.

Abby, touched by her account, perceived the contagious energy. The room resonated with her fervor, and their dialogue became a celebration of the craft they loved. Clara and Alex's quiet exchanges became a cherished routine. They anticipated their secluded corner each day, where their unspoken melodies wove a silent concerto.

Clara arrived at their designated spot, her violin cradled against her chest. Alex sat poised at the piano with his notebook, ready to translate her imaginary tunes into resonant chords.

Their performances became a source of highlight in the hospital. Clara's eyes sparkled with excitement, her fingers poised over the violin strings, ready to conjure melodies from the depths of her soul. Alex's expressions were focused as he awaited Clara's invisible cues.

Their sessions resonated with an emotional depth that transcended spoken language. Clara's movements, her bow gliding over the strings, weave intricate tales. Alex responded kindly, his fingers dancing across the keys.

Curious onlookers slowly gathered around, drawn by the haunting beauty of their musical dialogue.

The room transformed into an intimate concert hall. Anticipation built as more people settled in. The footsteps approaching and chairs shifting blended with the violin and piano.

They, oblivious to the growing audience, continued their performance. The room was filled with residents and staff members. The sounds of hushed conversations and shuffling footsteps merged, adding to the electric atmosphere charged with expectation.

The last notes and a thunderous wave of applause erupted from the audience. The sound reverberated through the room.

Smiles illuminated faces, and eyes shimmered with appreciation, the collective reaction painting a portrait of heartfelt awe.

Surrounded by exhilaration and humble gratitude, Clara glanced around, absorbing their music's profound impact on the crowd. The sights of faces lit up with emotion, and the sounds of applause interwoven with whispered expressions of amazement and excitement in the air.

Clara's heart swelled with pride, fulfillment, and a profound sense of accomplishment. The room buzzed with a collective outpouring of appreciation and admiration.

The applause subsided, and Clara and Alex exchanged gentle smiles. The room was aglow with the lingering warmth of their song, an indelible impression etched into the hearts of all who witnessed their performance.

Abby approached Clara with a soft smile, her eyes shimmering, "It's hard to believe your time here has ended. You've made incredible progress."

Clara nodded, a wistful smile gracing her lips. "It's surreal to leave. This place was a second home, and the people here, a second family."

"You've left a mark. Your sessions with Alex inspired everyone," Abby said, her voice tinged with admiration.

"It was more than music," she murmured, her eyes reflecting gratitude. "It was a language, a bond between us."

"You both created something beautiful."

"You, Abby, have been an anchor throughout," she remarked.

"It's been an honor," Abby replied, enveloping Clara in a heartfelt embrace. "You'll be missed, but your spirit will remain here, inspiring others on their journeys."

She scanned the center's familiar corners, seeking Alex in his usual spot by the piano. He was nowhere to be found. A knot of worry tightened in her chest as she approached the staff.

"Excuse me, have you seen Alex?" Clara inquired.

The staff exchanged somber glances, one of them stepping forward. "I'm sorry. Alex passed away in his sleep last night," they said.

The news hit her like a sudden storm. The sights around her blurred with the tears in her eyes. Clara's world felt suspended, trapped between the weight of the news and the disbelief that Alex, her companion and friend, was not nearby. Sorrow hung in the air, a poignant reminder of the fragility of life.

She grappled with the reality of Alex's absence, and her emotions intensified—a tumultuous cacophony of sorrow and a haunting silence that enveloped her in its embrace. The room was colder, echoing the void left behind by Alex's sudden departure.

After Alex's passing, Clara stood amidst the quiet corridors of the rehabilitation center, her heart heavy with a profound sense of loss. Memories of their silent sessions flooded her, each note they never played together ringing through her mind.

She was drawn to the piano, where Alex had created symphonies without a word. Her fingers trembled over the keys, and a melody emerged—one born from the depths of her soul, a tribute to the unspoken bond they shared. Clara rose from the piano bench with a heavy heart; her soul lay bare through the music. She understood that while Alex may not be present, the echoes of their conversations and the melodies would forever resonate with her.

Clara reflected on how she had once lost her violin ability, feeling like a vital part of herself had vanished. Yet, in that loss, she discovered an unexpected healing through music. She felt a sense of peace as she remembered the solace she had found in melodies. She bid farewell to her cherished companion with a faint smile touched by sadness. Carrying the melodies of their friendship with her, she stepped forward, embracing the uncertain path ahead, forever shaped by the silent yet profound bond that had guided her through her healing journey.

The Gift of Time

S cott Taylor is a man defined by his ambition. He is a dedicated businessman. His days are full of meetings, conference calls, and strategic planning sessions as he oversees a diverse portfolio of client projects. From scale infrastructure developments to intricate financial analyses, Scott's expertise and leadership are indispensable to the success of each endeavor.

He orchestrates every aspect of the project lifecycle, from initial conception to final delivery. Scott collaborates with cross-functional teams, including engineers, analysts, and designers, to ensure that milestones are met and client expectations are exceeded.

Scott thrives on the challenges it presents. He thrives in high-pressure environments, leveraging his sharp analytical skills and strong decision-making abilities to navigate complex problems and find innovative solutions. Each task was an opportunity to impact and leave a legacy in business and beyond.

He dug deeper into his work, and his relationship with his family began to suffer. His wife, Karly, often expressed irritation at his long hours and absence from important household celebrations.

Scott was torn between his desire to provide a comfortable life for his family and his desire to spend quality time with them. He found himself trapped in a constant struggle. He yearned to be around for his children's milestones. He wanted to attend their soccer games and school plays, but the pressures of his occupation always took precedence.

He climbed the corporate ladder. His vocational ambitions soared while his focus on his family waned. With each promotion and accolade, he devoted more time to his work, believing his sacrifices would benefit his loved ones. However, as his job expectations increased, Scott began to understand the toll it was taking on his relationships at home.

At first, it was subtle—skipped meals, postponed vacations, and hurried phone talks to his children before bedtime. Time passed. The divide between his professional aspirations and his familial responsibilities grew wider. Scott found himself distant from Karly and their girls. The intimacy and warmth of their lives faded into the background of his busy job.

One day, Jacob, a coworker, spotted him looking distracted.

"Hey, everything okay?" Jacob asked, concern evident in his voice.

"Karly is at it again. This time because I missed Julia's soccer game," Scott replied with a sigh. "I told them I needed to finish his project, but she just gave me a look and walked away."

"I grasp it, man. Balancing work and family isn't easy. Have you talked to your boss about it?"

"I'm afraid to. I don't want to seem unable to handle the workload."

"You should talk to him. Your family comes first, Scott."

"Yeah, you're right. Thanks, Jacob."

Jacob's words struck a chord with him. He had always believed he prioritized his family, but now he questioned whether that was the case. Determined, he decided that something had to alter—his job or his family. He prayed it wouldn't be the latter.

Breaking free from his job's grip would require courage and sacrifice, two qualities he wasn't sure he possessed.

Sitting alone in his home office, surrounded by stacks of paperwork and the soft glow of his computer screen, he glanced at the family photos on the walls. A pang of regret washed over him. How had his girls grown up?

Scott looked at them. He missed so much of their lives, buried under the weight of his work.

He made a silent vow to himself. He would find a way to make up for wasted time, to be the father his girls deserved. He wiped away a tear and prayed that it was not too late to reclaim the bond they once shared.

"Have you realized how fast the girls are growing up?" Scott sighed, his gaze fixed on a family photo on the wall. "Olivia's already a sophomore, and Juliet's in 8th grade. Yesterday, they were little girls."

"Time does fly. They're developing into such wonderful young women."

Scott's shoulders slumped as he spoke, evident in the tightness of his jaw and the exasperated sighs that punctuated his sentences. "I can't believe how much I've missed. All these late nights at the office, all the soccer games, and school functions. It's like I blinked, and they were teenagers."

She gently placed her hand on his arm, her touch warm and reassuring. "Honey," she said softly, her voice a soothing balm, "You're doing all this for our family. You're providing for us, giving us opportunities we wouldn't have otherwise."

Scott's shoulders sagged. "I wonder if it's worth it. I'm missing so much and can't gain that time."

Karly reached out to take his hand, her touch grounding him. "It's okay. We'll find a way to make up for lost time. Maybe we can plan some family outings or meals together. The girls understand how hard you're working for us."

Scott offered a small smile. "Thanks. I needed to talk about it. I want to be there for them more than anything."

She squeezed his hand. "I get you do. You will be. We'll overcome through this together."

He made a conscious decision to reevaluate his priorities. He recognized that reclaiming the closeness and connection he lost with his family would require sacrifice and effort. The price he was willing to pay. A sense of hope and renewal washed over him. He comprehended that true fulfillment lay not in professional success, but in the love and encouragement of those closest to him.

The following week passed in a blur. The days slipped by in much the same way as before. He tried to be more involved at home, attending his daughters' activities and making time for suppers, but the familiar work routine still dominated his life.

He sat down, frustrated. Things remained much the same as before. His job expectations continued to encroach on his time, leaving him frustrated and powerless to enact the change he so desired.

Scott couldn't overcome the regret. The status quo remained unchanged. Amidst his disappointment, a hope emerged - tomorrow was his birthday. He viewed it as an opportunity for a fresh start. Reaffirming his promise to his family and making the necessary changes to prioritize them was possible. He resolved to make his birthday the beginning of a new chapter, where his family came first above all else.

Olivia and Juliet sat cozily in the living room, sunlight filtering through the curtains, casting a warm glow around them. Olivia, with a thoughtful expression, broke the silence.

"Hey, Juliet, Dad's birthday is coming up soon," she began, turning to her younger sister.

Juliet looked up from her book, her eyes brightening with interest. "Oh yeah, we should do something nice for him," she agreed eagerly.

Olivia nodded, a smile playing on her lips. " How about we surprise him with a special breakfast on his birthday?" she suggested.

Juliet's face lit up with excitement. "That's a great idea! Dad always says your pancakes are his favorite," she exclaimed.

Olivia chuckled softly. "Yeah, he does love my pancakes. We could make pancakes, bacon, and his favorite coffee," she added, imagining his smile.

Juliet clapped her hands lightly. "We could set the table with his favorite fruit and juice. He'll be so happy," she said, picturing the surprise.

Olivia smiled warmly at her sister. "I can already see his face when he wakes up to a special birthday breakfast," she said, filled with anticipation.

Juliet nodded enthusiastically. "He's going to love it. Thanks for doing this with me," she said gratefully.

Olivia reached out and squeezed Juliet's hand. "Of course, Juliet. Dad deserves the best. Let's make his birthday morning one to remember,"

When morning arrived, Olivia and Juliet rose early to prepare pancakes and bacon. They arranged the pancakes and fruit on a platter. They giggled while creating a crafted note with colorful drawings of family celebrations and heartfelt messages.

"Happy birthday, Dad!" they exclaimed, entering his room, excitement shining in their eyes. Their smiles widened as he read their words while presenting the tray and card.

"We made breakfast for you," Olivia said, her voice filled with pride.

"We hope you like it," Juliet added, her eyes sparkling.

"What's this?" he asked, a smile on his face.

"We made it for you," Juliet replied. "Go ahead, open it."

The card depicted family moments, like playing at the park, enjoying meals together, and capturing cherished memories.

Scott's eyes welled with tears. "I love it," he said, embracing his daughters.

"We love you, Daddy," Olivia said, knowing his need.

After giving Scott a quick kiss, the girls headed out. Scott felt a pang of guilt for working on a Saturday, but he promised himself he'd make it up to them with some quality time soon.

Karly found Scott sitting at the dining table, his face reflective. "Happy birthday," she said, leaning in to kiss him before sitting beside him. "What's on your mind?"

Scott sighed, showing her the drawings. "The girls created these for me. Why am I going to work today? I need time with all of you."

Karly's heart ached at the weariness in Scott's voice. Placing a gentle hand on his, she stared into his eyes. "We're all fine. We'll figure something out together. Your family comes first. Always."

Olivia thought about how to make her dad's birthday. Memories rushed back from her time at cheerleading camp. She remembered how she made a coupon book for the other girls to spend time together during the week. They bonded over activities like ice cream or having a movie night.

With a stack of colorful paper and markers spread out before them, they began giggling and chatting as they decorated each page. They reminisced about past family outings and shared their hopes for the future, bonding over their love for their dad.

Thrilled about their plan, she approached her younger sister, Juliet, to discuss the ticket book they wanted to make for their dad's birthday. Sitting down together, they brainstormed different ideas, eager to create memorable experiences for their family.

They reflected on their choices, and Juliet asked, "Do you think Dad will like the ticket book we made?"

Olivia nodded. "I think so! He's always talking about spending more time together as a family."

"I hope so. We put a lot of thought into each coupon."

Sharing her sister's sentiment, she chimed in, "Me too. I can't wait to watch his reaction when he opens it."

Their anticipation grew as they discussed their plans for later. "We can take him out to supper tonight, just like Mom told us," Olivia suggested.

Juliet grinned in agreement. "Yeah, that'll be fun! I can't wait!"

As he stepped into the office, Scott's mind raced with the day's tasks, but beneath the surface, a pang of guilt tugged at him. He couldn't shake the memory of Olivia and Juliet's homemade birthday gifts. Their effort to connect with him reminded him of the precious moments he often missed. Despite his dedication to his career, he couldn't deny the growing sense that something crucial was slipping away.

Amidst the hectic pace of the day, he found himself immersed in his tasks, the significance of the date slipping his mind. The hours passed, and the office's bustle and job demands clouded his brain. It pushed any notion of his birthday to the back of his mind.

Caught up in the rhythm of his work, Scott failed to spot the passing of time. The act of kindness his girls prepared for him was a distant memory buried beneath the weight of his professional responsibilities. With each passing hour, he became more engrossed in his work, focusing on the tasks.

As Scott wrapped up his tasks for the day, Mr. Johnson interrupted him and invited him into his office. Once inside, Mr. Johnson commended Scott on his exceptional performance, praising his hard work and commitment to the company's goals.

"Scott, I've been impressed with your dedication. Your efforts have not gone unnoticed, and I believe you're ready for the next step in your career."

Scott's chest puffed up with pride as he straightened his posture. "Thank you, sir," he said, his voice steady but warm. "I appreciate the opportunity to contribute to the company's success."

Mr. Johnson leaned forward. "I've been considering you for a raise with a significant pay increase. It would involve more responsibility and hours, including travel that would take you away from home for stretches at a time."

Scott's initial excitement dimmed as he sat down, the weight of the promotion sinking in. His fingers drummed nervously on the chair's armrest, and his brows wrinkled in thought. He glanced around the office, taking in the new responsibilities that now seemed to loom over him, the thrill of success mingling with a flicker of apprehension. The prospect of a higher salary was enticing, but he couldn't ignore the toll it would take on his family life. Memories of his daughters' thoughtful birthday gestures flooded his mind.

"I'm honored, Mr. Johnson," Scott began, hesitating. "I need to consider how this would impact my family. They mean everything to me, and I don't want to sacrifice too much time away from them."

Mr. Johnson nodded. "I understand. It's a big decision, and family should always come first. Take time to think it over and tell me what you decide. Whatever you choose, I have no doubt you'll continue to excel in your career."

Scott gave a grateful nod and left the meeting. As he walked down the hallway, his steps slowed, and he rubbed the back of his neck. His mind swirled with conflicting feelings, the pride of his promotion mixing with a knot of uncertainty in his stomach. The prospect of advancement was tempting, but he recognized he needed to prioritize his family above all else.

At the end of the workday, he collected his belongings, suddenly struck by guilt for overlooking his birthday. Regret and disappointment overwhelmed him like a wave crashing over.

He pulled out his phone and dialed Karly's number. Her voice welcomed him, and he couldn't help but smile. "How was your day, honey?" she asked.

"It was productive. What time was our reservation at the restaurant?" As the words left his mouth, his mood shifted. "I can't wait to hug you all," he added, his tone softening.

"We can't wait to celebrate with you!" Karly exclaimed. "Forty is a monumental year," she teased, eliciting a chuckle from him.

"Well, you're not too far behind. I'll retrieve the black for you," he joked back, imagining her playful grin on the other end of the line.

He experienced Karly's warmth radiating through the phone as she responded, "I'm just about home, sweetheart."

"Drive safe, and come home to us," Karly added.

With a contented grin, Scott ended the call. Karly had always been his pillar of support, standing by him. He understood he was a fortunate man, blessed with a beautiful family.

A wave of smiles met him. The girls dressed in their finest attire, thrilled for the evening ahead. Karly welcomed him with a kiss, and Scott felt a rush of warmth spread through his chest. The affectionate gesture melted away the day's stress. Her kiss reminded him of what truly mattered, and he couldn't help but smile, feeling more at peace.

"Hi, birthday boy," Karly welcomed him with a flirtatious smirk.

Olivia's eyes lit up as she ran to him, wrapping her arms around his waist. "We've been waiting for you to come home all day!" she exclaimed, her voice filled with excitement. "We hope you like where we're taking you for supper and what we've got for you!" She glanced up at him with a hopeful smile.

Juliet joined in, Juliet chimed in, her voice bubbling with happiness. She bounced on her toes, her eyes sparkling with excitement, her joy radiating through her every word. "Yeah, we can't wait to show you everything!"

"Let's all climb in the car and head out," Karly urged.

They journeyed to the restaurant. Scott glanced at Olivia and Juliet through the rearview mirror, a curious smile on his lips. "So, what did you girls do all day?" he asked.

Olivia exchanged a secretive glance with Juliet before turning to Scott with a mischievous grin. "Sorry, Dad," she replied with a playful wink. "We can't tell you. It's a surprise."

Juliet giggled, adding fuel to the intrigue. "Yeah, it's a secret," she chimed in, her eagerness contained.

Scott chuckled, feigning disappointment. "Well, I guess I'll have to wait," he glanced at Karly with a knowing smile.

They rolled up to the restaurant. Scott kicked things off with a playful jab, "Hope y'all brought your wallets 'cause I'm starving!

"Dad, Mom's got us covered!" Juliet teased, setting off a round of laughter.

They piled out of the car, each girl grabbing her dad's hand while Karly brought up the rear.

"We are on time," Karly remarked, noting how the girls clung to their dad despite growing up. They strolled into the restaurant and approached the hostess stand, where Karly spotted a name tag that read "Bethany."

"Welcome to Gibson's!" chirped the hostess with a grin. "Got a reservation?"

"Yep," Karly confirmed with a grin. "Taylor, party of 4!

The hostess looked up. "An occasion?

Leaning in conspiratorially, Karly whispered, "Oh, you bet. It's his 40th birthday. Please embarrass him. Got it, Bethany?" she added, winking.

"Right this way," she replied with a chuckle, leading them to their table. The ambiance was upscale, with soft lighting and elegant tablecloths setting the mood. Everyone settled in, ready for the festivities.

"So, what's everyone feeling' for dinner?" Scott asked, scanning the menu. "I'm thinking a juicy steak.

The girls giggled, knowing their dad's predictable order of BBQ chicken. The waitress arrived to take their orders. She asked, "What can I bring y'all tonight? "I'll take the mac 'n' cheese," Juliet piped up.

"I'll have the petite steak salad," Olivia said.

Karly turned to the server and placed her order, "I'll have the smoked salmon."

Scott followed suit, "I'll stick with the usual," he said, eliciting giggles from the girls.

Juliet exchanged a knowing look with Olivia, "I knew it."

Dinner progressed, and conversation flowed about their recent Girls' Day activities and plans for the week ahead.

"I've got a soccer game on Tuesday and a band concert on Thursday," Juliet announced.

Olivia sighed, "I've got a cheerleading meeting on Monday, an ASB meeting on Wednesday, and a basketball game to cheer at on Friday. Kind of a light week."

Scott raised an eyebrow. "Sounds like you're juggling quite a bit." Glancing at Karly, he remarked, "We've got something going on every day."

"An average week," Karly reassured him with a smile.

Scott realized that the whole family was mirroring his packed schedule, recognizing that their precious family time was slipping away. The server cleared the dinner plates, and smiles spread across the table.

"Dad," Olivia began, "we've been working hard all day on your birthday gift. It's something for all of us. You work hard, but we wanted to give you the most valuable thing we have—our time."

Scott's eyes welled up as he looked around, his voice catching in his throat. "Wow," he managed to say, his voice trembling slightly. "This means the world to me." His gaze softened with gratitude, and he took a deep breath, visibly moved by the thoughtful gesture.

Juliet said, "It's a coupon book of activities together. There's one for bowling, a walk around the block, and a movie night. You even pick the movie, and we'll provide the popcorn."

"How did you understand I needed this?" Scott asked, looking at Karly. "Did you put them up to this?"

Karly smiled and shook her head. "Nope, they came up with it all on their own," she said, glancing at the girls. "It's such a sweet and thoughtful gift, girls."

"It is," Scott agreed, pulling the girls into a warm hug.

*** (New scene)

Pulling into the driveway and the garage, the girls hopped out of the car.

"Good night, Dad," Olivia said, pausing at the doorstep.

"Thanks. It's the best gift anyone gave me," Scott replied.

"You're welcome," the girls chorused, flashing smiles before disappearing into the house.

"They're wonderful," Scott remarked, looking at Karly.

"They sure are," Karly agreed, returning his smile. "They adore their father." she headed inside, leaving Scott to bask in the warmth of his daughters' love.

Scott trudged up the stairs. He paused momentarily at the doorway, his shoulders slumped, and his gaze fixed on the floor. He moved slowly, his posture tense, and he sighed deeply before finally crossing the threshold.

Karly was already involved in her nightly routine, brushing her teeth and setting her skincare products on the vanity.

Karly turned from the vanity, her smile fading to concern as she listened intently to Scott's words.

"What is it, honey?" she inquired, her eyes searching his face.

"I've been offered a promotion," Scott revealed, meeting Karly's gaze.

Karly's excitement dimmed as she noticed Scott's somber mood. She walked over and sat beside him, placing a comforting hand on his arm. "Are you excited about it?" she asked softly, her voice filled with concern.

Scott's face tightened as a deep frown settled on his brow. His usually bright eyes darkened. His shoulders sagged, and he ran a hand through his hair, the weight of his emotions visible in his weary posture. "That's because it involves a significant amount of travel. I'll be away on business trips four days a week."

Karly settled on the edge of the bed. "Wow," she breathed. "That's a lot of time away from us. What did you tell him?"

"I said I needed to discuss it with you first, but I'm inclined to accept," Scott admitted.

Her smile faded, replaced by a furrowed brow. "What is the start date?" she inquired.

"In a month," Scott replied. "It's a chance for advancement."

Karly's expression turned somber. "Did you see how happy the girls were tonight just having you there?" she asked. "They want to be with you. Their schedules are starting to mirror yours because they witness how it's become a part of your life, Scott."

Sitting down beside her, he sighed. "I understand, but I didn't grasp it until now. After their gift tonight, I'm unsure if I can go through with it."

"What if you decline? What other options do you have?"

"I'm not sure. It might limit my chances for future promotions," he admitted.

"Would that be so terrible?" Then, she retreated to her side of the bed and slipped under the covers.

Monday came, and Scott replayed the conversation Karly and he had. Since that night, it has been hard to concentrate, knowing she is mad at him and wants him to say no to the promotion. Just then, his administrative assistant walked in the door.

"Here are the reports you asked for." She said with a smile.

Scott took them from her, "Thank you."

Scott returned to work before he perceived it was the end of the day. He was getting ready to leave the coupon book his girls made for his birthday tucked in his briefcase. He thumbed through it, and the ticket for a movie night caught his eye.

"Time is the greatest gift that a person can give to another. I need to do things with them. They won't be around forever," he said to himself.

Scott arrived home and called out a greeting, but there was no response. Remembering the family activities scheduled for the evening, he realized he was alone. He went upstairs to the home office and resumed working on his project, engrossed in his tasks. Unaware of the passage of time, he didn't realize when the others arrived home. Juliet entered the office and bid him goodnight with a hug and a kiss on the cheek so that he became aware of their presence.

Karly joined him, sitting beside him and wrapping her arm around him. "Scott, you provide so well for this family, and I love you, but I want you to reconsider taking this promotion. I don't detect any upside to it," she said.

Scott sighed, removing his glasses. "I'm not sure if I want to take it. It's a new role, and I feel stuck in my responsibilities. I need to take it to figure out what I want in my career," he explained.

Standing up, Karly walked over to the doorway and paused. "You find out soon, or those girls will grow up and start their own families. You will have missed it all," she said, her words filled with love but carrying a weight of urgency.

A wave of confusion washed over him. He needed clarity, a chance to discern whether he was making the right decision.

In the following weeks, life continued at its usual hectic pace for Scott and his family. Immersed in his work, time seemed to slip unnoticed.

Scott prepared for his upcoming promotion, tying up loose ends and preparing for the transition. He stumbled upon the girl's gift. A wave of regret washed over him. He stared at it, his shoulders slumping. Once a source of excitement, the forgotten gift now seemed to carry a weight of missed moments and unfulfilled promises. Memories of conversations with Karly resurfaced, reminding him of the precious moments he risked missing out on if things didn't change.

A steely resolve took hold of him. His grip tightened around the cover, and his eyes sharpened with newfound clarity. He stood up with a determined stride, realizing that it wasn't too late to shift his focus, prioritizing his family over work.

Scott's mind was a whirl as he drove home, his gaze fixed on the road ahead. The work phone was left behind, forgotten in the rush.

At the store, he moved through the aisles with a sense of purpose, grabbing soda, candy, chips, and popcorn, his cart filling up with a junk food feast. He then picked up several pizzas, the scent of warm cheese and pepperoni mingling with the other items in his cart. He dialed his wife's number as he loaded the last groceries into his car.

"Hello?" she answered.

"Hi honey, tell the girls they can't go anywhere tonight."

"Why?" Karly asked.

"It's a secret."

"I'll tell them they're confined to the house. Maybe I'll say they're in trouble to add a bit of drama," she said, laughing.

"Don't make them too nervous. I'll be home soon," Scott replied.

"Okay, I'll wait for you," Karly said, smiling as she hung up.

Moments later, he walked through the door, calling out for the girls. "Olivia, Juliette, come down here."

"What is it?" Olivia asked as she descended the stairs. "Is it pizza?"

"Go into the family room, and I'll fill you in," her dad replied.

Juliette followed close behind. "What is it, Daddy?"

"Follow your sister, sweetheart," Scott said with a smile.

With everyone in the family room, he made his announcement. "I'm using my first birthday coupon. Tonight, we're having a family movie night."

The girls' smiles widened, but there was a flicker of concern in their eyes. They exchanged glances, a hint of uncertainty casting shadows on their excited expressions.

"What about work? Won't they call?"

"If they do, they'll be calling my desk drawer. I left my work phone at the office. You, your sister, and your mom have me for the whole weekend," he answered.

Karly, Olivia, and Juliette couldn't believe it. A weekend without the work phone was a rare event. Scott told them about the pizza and the junk food, saying they could have as much as they wanted. The girls giggled as they headed to the kitchen to grab dinner before Karly could leave.

"I want to talk with you before we sleep tonight," Scott told Karly.

She smiled and responded, "Another surprise? You've outdone yourself tonight. Who are you, and where did you take my husband?"

The movie was a romcom, something the girls wanted to view, but none of their friends would see it with them. The night was filled with soda, licorice, popcorn, and chocolate.

"Are you enjoying yourselves?" Scott asked.

"Yes," Juliette said. "I think I am going to be on a sugar high for the next week. Thank you, Daddy. I am having lots of fun."

Olivia added, "I loved the movie. I can't remember the last time we had this much fun together. I hope we can do this more often but without all the food. A girl must monitor her figure."

Both Karly and Scott laughed. "I am glad you all had fun. I enjoyed it, too, and I can't wait to do more with you. I have lots more tickets in this book, so prepare for bowling tomorrow!"

"I can't wait," said Juliette. "I might not do so well, but being with you and Mom will be fun."

The girls went to bed, leaving Mom and Dad to clean up the evening's mess. Karly gazed at Scott and said, "Let's leave this for tomorrow. What did you want to tell me?" she asked.

Scott sat down beside her and took a deep breath. "I want to quit my job."

"What??" she said.

"Listen! I have lots of vacation time. Eight weeks saved up. I want to start my own business. I'll do the same work but for myself. I'll be home more, and we can have more nights like this."

"I will support you in anything you decide," she said. "Having you home more would be a welcome change, but I think we can adjust," she said with a smile.

"It is wonderful to hear that. I can start planning and do it while the children are asleep, so it doesn't take up our family time."

They went upstairs, both with a twinkle in their eyes.

Scott woke up early the next morning, eager to start working on his business ideas. Financing would be necessary, but he didn't want to risk losing money that could impact his family. Business always involves risk. He protected the house and other assets.

A noise at his office door caught his attention. Olivia stood there, watching her father work. She wanted to say something but didn't want to disturb him.

"Good morning, sweetheart," Scott said, motioning her into the office.

"I just wanted to tell you how much I enjoyed last night's family night," Olivia said, tears forming. "It's been a long time since we did anything as a family, and it was fun to laugh together. We made a wonderful memory."

"It was a great memory for me, too," Scott said, hugging his eldest daughter. "I promise we will have more of them before you go to college."

"I hope so," she said, heading for the stairs.

Scott's shoulders relaxed, and a small, relieved smile tugged at his lips. He took a deep breath, and a contented warmth spread through him, confirming he was on the right path. He began typing his resignation letter. He kept it short and simple, explaining that he wanted more time for his family. He believed he could succeed on his own. His drive remained strong, but now he could set his hours and be there for his wife and girls. The exchange with Olivia confirmed his decision.

He finished the letter, closed his laptop, and took out his phone. Arrangements for a family bowling night at a trendy place followed.

Monday arrived, and Scott entered his office building, feeling nervous and exhilarated. "Today is the day," he told himself. He made his way to his boss's office and smiled. "I'm afraid I can't accept the promotion," he said.

His boss stared him in the eye. "Oh, why not, Scott? You've earned it and are the best person for this position."

"Thank you for those kind words. They mean a lot, coming from someone I respect. I've been doing a lot of soul-searching over the past few months. The greatest gift I received came from my daughters on my birthday. They want to spend time with me. They need me, and I need to spend more time with them. I don't want to miss life's important event."

"I understand," his boss replied. "Is there any way I can get you to change your mind? I don't want to lose you."

"No, my mind is made up. How do you want me to proceed with the transition?" Scott asked.

"I'll start succession planning this morning and let you know how you can help. Go ahead and let your team know," his boss said.

He worked throughout the day with renewed purpose, feeling sharper and more focused. The anticipation of telling his daughters kept him motivated. Five o'clock arrived. He gathered his things and left the office, eager to share the news.

He grabbed his phone and dialed a familiar number. "Hello, Karly? I'm on my way home. Please make sure the girls are there, too. I want to tell them about my job."

"I'm sure they will be excited to listen to everything you have to say," she responded.

"Please don't let them in on it, Karly. I want to be the one to tell them," Scott asked.

Karly responded, "OK, hunny. I won't say a thing. You'll be able to hear their excitement miles away."

"Alright, sweetheart. I'll see you soon," Scott said.

Scott took a deep breath and continued home. He didn't know the future but had faith in his family. These two things would see him through, and he knew everything would be alright.

He pulled into the driveway, gathered his belongings, and headed inside. Olivia studied at the dining room table, books and papers spread out, highlighting and making notes. Scott stood there for a minute, soaking it in. Soon, this scene would no longer be part of his daily life, and he knew he would miss her when she went away to college.

"Hi, Olivia," Scott said to her.

"Hi, Daddy," she said with a smile. "You're home early."

"I know, and I have something to tell you and your sister. I'll go up and change, then get her to come downstairs," he said, returning her smile.

Olivia returned to her books, and Scott began to walk upstairs. At the top, Juliet was watching TV and noticed him standing there.

"Hi, Daddy. You're home early. Is everything okay?" she asked.

"Everything is better than fine, sweetie. I need you to go downstairs in a minute. I have something to tell both you and your sister."

"Ok," she responded, getting up and descending the stairs.

Scott went into his bedroom, changed out of his tie and shirt, and put on a T-shirt and jeans. He glanced in the mirror and took a deep sigh. This marked the beginning, and the more people he told about his plans, the more accountable he would become. At this point, there was no turning back. Scott began to walk downstairs and heard laughter from the living room.

The girls were laughing at something on Olivia's phone.

"What are you watching?" Scott asked.

Olivia responded, "It's just a funny video. What did you want to tell us, Dad? It must be important for you to be home early."

"I think it is important," Scott answered. I'm just going to say it."

"Mom is pregnant," Juliet said, starting to laugh.

"No, I am not pregnant," Karly's voice came from the dining room as she appeared in the doorway.

Scott glanced back at Karly and smiled. "Spending time with you two has been some of the best times of my life. You both have taught me that time is the most important thing in a family. I don't want to miss out on anything in your life. I quit my job."

"Really???" Juliet exclaimed. "Does this mean you will be around more? You will be home for dinners, my games, and activities?"

Olivia appeared concerned. "What are you going to do for work? Are we going to be okay?"

"We will be fine," Scott assured them. "I've discussed this with your mom, and we have planned it all out."

They all got up and hugged, smiling as they left the room. Karly approached Scott and put her arms around him.

"I'm so glad you've made this decision. I love you," Karly said.

"I love you too," Scott responded.

Scott went to the back patio and sat in one of the chairs. Karly soon joined him, bringing him something to drink. She sat down in the chair next to him and grabbed his hand. They sat there in silence. Scott took a deep breath and sighed, feeling content. Karly squeezed his hand.

Scott gazed at the setting sun, its golden light casting long shadows. As he watched, memories of laughter and shared moments with his girls played in his mind—picking them up from school, their giggles during movie nights, and the warmth of their hugs. Each image brought a smile to his face. He took in the scene around him, feeling the weight of the day lift. His girls gave him the best gift ever: the gift of time.

The Last Dance

Rose and James had been married for over six decades. Today, they returned to the grand ballroom, which holds the essence of their story. The once-glorious hall, with its high ceilings and ornate chandeliers, stood as an example of their enduring love.

Rose walked through the familiar doors, and nostalgia surrounded her. The opulent grandeur of the ballroom seemed to shimmer with the echoes of their past. She traced her fingers along the elegant moldings, and the soft glow of the chandeliers brought back vivid memories of youthful exuberance and laughter that once filled the room. The gentle touch of James's hand in hers felt like a comforting thread connecting her to those tender moments, as if no time had passed since their wedding day.

Returning to the ballroom brought back many memories, including the first time they met. It happened at a small, bustling café. She worked behind the counter, serving coffee with a warm smile that seemed to light up the whole café. Every day, James walked in and ordered the same thing, but it wasn't just the coffee he craved. He looked forward to their brief conversations, savoring the sound of her voice that made each visit feel like a small, comforting ritual. Her smile was a beacon in his day, and the routine of their exchanges was a cherished highlight he eagerly anticipated.

Her laughter rang through the café like a melody, drawing smiles from everyone around. Her eyes crinkled with genuine warmth each time she spoke, and her thoughtful gestures, like remembering customers' names and their favorite orders, spoke volumes of her kindness.

He approached the counter, smiling. "Another black coffee and apple pie, please."

She nodded, her eyes sparkling. "Coming right up. How's your day going?"

"I'm better now," he said, his gaze steady on hers. What's your favorite book?"

She paused, considering. "Pride and Prejudice. Yours?"

"To Kill a Mockingbird," James replied. "Why Pride and Prejudice?"

"The characters are real," she explained. "What about Mockingbird?"

He shrugged. "The message. It stays with you."

Rose handed him his coffee and pie. "Good choice," she said, smiling.

James took the plate, his fingers brushing hers. "Thanks. See you tomorrow?"

"Same time," she replied, her smile lingering as he found his seat.

They began to meet at the café, sharing stories and dreams. He admired Rose's intelligence and gentle nature. She was drawn to his wit and how he made her special.

James listened as Rose spoke of her favorite books and travel dreams. "I'd love to go to Paris someday," she said, her eyes bright.

"You'll get there," he replied, confident in his voice. "I can imagine you walking along the Seine."

She laughed. "What dreams do you have?"

He thought for a moment. "I dream of writing a story that means something," he confessed.

Rose nodded, understanding. "You will," she said. "Your words touch lives."

They did so through the stories he revealed and the advice he gave. He had a knack for listening and understanding people's struggles. Friends often turned to him for guidance, finding comfort in his wisdom.

At the café, James leaned over the counter, his expression earnest as he listened to the young man's concerns about his career. With a thoughtful nod, he shared his journey, recounting the twists and turns that had led him to where he was now. His words, filled with personal anecdotes and encouragement, seemed to light up the young man's face, offering him a new perspective and hope for what might lie ahead.

She saw this in him. Their exchanges at the café filled with dreams of the future and the impact he hoped to have through his writing.

They spent hours like this, lost in conversation. The café became their haven, a place where they could be themselves.

He had a dry wit, often delivering remarks with a straight face.

James said, stirring his coffee, "I once tried to be a baker."

Rose raised an eyebrow. "How did that go?"

"I kneaded the dough," he deadpanned, causing her to laugh.

His humor ranged from puns to witty observations about everyday life, always delivered with impeccable timing.

He spoke of resilience, finding beauty in adversity, and the importance of kindness in a world that sometimes seemed harsh. Rose listened, captivated by his perspective.

"Life's like an adventure. We face obstacles, but they shape us into who we're meant to be." James said.

"That's so true. Sometimes, it's hard to discover the beauty amidst the struggles."

"It's there if you look. Like a flower blooming amid a storm,".

"I love that analogy. It's a reminder to always look for the silver lining," Rose said.

"And kindness? It's like a light in the darkness. It can change someone's whole world."

"I couldn't agree more. It keeps us going, even when things are bleak."

Their conversation flowed, touching on resilience, finding beauty in adversity, and the transformative power of kindness.

Words flowed between them, building a new and timeless link.

"I have something to tell you," James said.

She looked up, her heart pounding. "What is it?"

He took a deep breath. "I've realized something. I've fallen for you."

Rose's cheeks flushed, her eyes widening in surprise. "James, I... I feel the same way."

They stood under the twinkling stars, their hearts racing with newfound understanding. Without another word, he leaned in, and their lips met in a loving kiss.

With his heart racing and his hands trembling with nervous anticipation, James knew he couldn't wait.

"There's something I've been wanting to ask you," he said, his voice trembling with nervous excitement.

She looked at him. "What is it?"

James took a deep breath, reaching for her hand. "Will you marry me?"

She gasped, her hand flying to her mouth in shock. "Yes, yes, a thousand times yes!"

They embraced, their hearts overflowing with love and joy, as they began to plan their future together.

Rose and James exchanged vows in an intimate outdoor ceremony surrounded by lush greenery and fragrant flowers. Their closest friends and family gathered under a canopy as Rose walked down the aisle, her eyes meeting James's, stirring a wave of emotion between them. The ceremony was simple yet profound, filled with heartfelt vows and touching moments. After sealing their vows with a kiss and exchanging rings, they were pronounced husband and wife, greeted by cheers that mingled with the birdsong and rustling leaves.

The reception that followed was lively, with laughter, elegant floral arrangements, and soft music filling the air. Guests toasted to the newlyweds' happiness and future as they danced the night away. From their initial meeting in a simple café, Rose and James's love had blossomed into a beautiful journey, culminating in their first dance as husband and wife in a grand ballroom, marking the beginning of their extraordinary adventure together.

Sixty years had passed since James and Rose shared their first dance as husband and wife in the grand ballroom. The memory of that moment remained etched in their hearts. They decided to revisit the floor where their marriage had begun to celebrate their diamond anniversary.

Rose wore her favorite dress. She held James' hand as he led her through the familiar doors. The chandeliers, though dimmed by time, still cast a gentle glow. Music from their youth was in the air.

They embarked on a journey, revisiting their early years together. From their whirlwind romance to raising a family, they reminisced about life's highs and lows.

"Let me tell you about when your grandfather and I went on a spontaneous road trip," she began. A twinkle in her eye as her children and grandchildren gathered around her.

"We didn't have a destination in mind, just each other's company and the open road ahead. We drove for hours, laughing and singing along to our favorite songs."

Her grandchildren leaned in, captivated by her words.

"Out of nowhere, we stumbled upon the most picturesque spot for a picnic," Rose continued. We spread our blanket, surrounded by nature's beauty, and enjoyed a simple meal together."

She paused, a fond smile tugging at her lips.

"It's moments like those that I treasure the most," she said. "The ones where it was just us, making moments that would last a lifetime."

James smiled. "Moments like those remind me why I fell in love with your grandmother." His voice was filled with love and admiration. "It wasn't about where we were or what we were doing, but being together, making experiences lasting a lifetime."

"Grandpa, did you and Grandma ever face any tough times when you were first married?" one of the grandchildren, Evan, asked.

He nodded, his expression thoughtful. "Oh, yes, we faced our fair share of difficulties," he replied. "There were times when money was tight, and we had to make sacrifices."

"Your grandmother and I always believed in facing those hurdles together," He proceeded, a note of determination in his tone. "We leaned on each other for support and found strength in our love."

He glanced at her, a soft smile playing on his lips.

"You know what?" he said, his voice filled with pride. "Those times only made us stronger as a couple. They taught us the true meaning of commitment and resilience and brought us closer together."

"That's right," Rose interjected, her gaze warm as she joined the conversation. Your grandfather and I learned early on that facing obstacles together only strengthened our relationship."

She reached out to squeeze his hand.

"You know what else?" she said as she sat down and looked him in the eye. "It's those difficulties that make the good times even sweeter. They remind us of what we've overcome and the strength we have as a family."

She smiled at Evan, caressing his cheek and her eyes shining with love and wisdom.

"So, remember," Rose concluded, her words carrying the weight of experience, "no matter what life throws your way, always lean on each other and face it together. That's the key to a happy and fulfilling life."

Sitting amidst their family, Rose's heart swelled with gratitude. These storytelling moments weren't just about reliving the past but passing down a legacy of love, resilience, and the simple joys they had cherished together. She hoped their children and grandchildren would understand the depth of their commitment.

"I remember when I was little," Sarah began a nostalgic smile across her face. "I had this big school project that I was nervous about."

"I didn't know where to start, but Mom and Dad were there for me every step of the way," Sarah persisted, her voice tinged with gratitude. "They helped me brainstorm ideas, stayed up late with me to work on it, and cheered me on when I presented it in class."

Tears glistened in their eyes as they listened to their daughter's words.

"It was a difficult project, but having Mom and Dad by my side made all the difference," Sarah concluded, reaching out to squeeze her parents' hands. "I'll never forget the love and support they've always given me."

"I remember one time," Hannah chimed in, a mischievous glint in her eyes, "when Dad decided to try his hand at cooking dinner."

The family chuckled, knowing James' culinary skills were, at best, questionable.

"He was determined to impress Mom with his gourmet skills," Hannah said, suppressing a giggle. "Let's just say things didn't go as planned."

The memory of James' culinary misadventure brought laughter as she recounted the hilarious mishaps.

"In the end," she concluded, shaking her head with amusement, "we ordered pizza and laughed about it. Dad may not be a master chef, but he knows how to keep us entertained!"

"Growing older," Rose began, her voice soft but laden with warmth, "life took on a different rhythm."

She glanced around at her family.

"We faced new hurdles and embraced new joys," she smiled tenderly. "Through it all, our love remained constant, a steady anchor in the ever-changing tides of life."

She squeezed James' hand.

"You all grew up and started families of your own," Rose said, her voice tinged with pride. "We gather here today. I couldn't be more grateful for the life we've enjoyed."

Tears shimmered in Rose's eyes.

James nodded, his gaze gentle as he picked up where she left off.

"We faced the difficulties of aging together," he said, his voice steady but filled with emotion. "With each passing year, our love only grew stronger."

He looked around at his family.

"We've shared countless recollections and milestones," he persisted, his smile reflecting the depth of his love. "Through it all, she had been my rock, constant companion, and greatest source of joy."

He reached out to wrap an arm around her, pulling her close.

"Now, as we celebrate sixty years of marriage surrounded by the love of our family," he concluded. His voice swelled with pride, "I can't help but feel like the luckiest man in the world."

"Family," she began, her voice carrying warmth and wisdom, "as your grandparents, your grandfather, and I have realized something important."

James nodded. "That's right," he added, "we've come to understand that while our days together are numbered, it's a reminder to live each moment to the fullest."

Their children and grandchildren listened.

"We've been blessed with a lifetime of love and recollections," Rose proceeded, her gaze sweeping over their family. "Now, as we celebrate sixty years of marriage, we're reminded of the importance of cherishing every precious moment we have together."

James smiled, his heart swelling with love for their family. "That's why we're here today," he said, his voice laden with gratitude, "to relive cherished experiences and create new ones together, surrounded by the love of our family."

They share a glance. With a gentle smile, he took Rose's hand, leading her onto the floor one last time. They moved closer, their love and connection unmistakable, guiding them through the timeless waltz of life.

They moved to the rhythm of the music. Rose nestled closer to James, feeling the steady beat of his heart against her own.

"James," she whispered, her voice audible, "do you remember our first dance here?"

James's eyes sparkled with nostalgia as he tightened his hold on her waist. "How could I forget?" he replied, an affectionate smile gracing his lips. "It seems like yesterday."

She sighed, her fingers tracing the lines of his face. "Time has flown by, hasn't it?" she murmured.

"It has," he agreed. "Every moment with you has been a treasure. I wouldn't trade it for anything."

Tears welled in Rose's eyes as she leaned in to rest her head against his chest. "Nor I," she whispered. "You've made my life complete."

They sway to the music, enveloped by the faded elegance of the ballroom, and memories of their youth flood back. The golden glow of the chandeliers casts a warm embrace over them, transporting them back to the day they shared their first dance as newlyweds.

Their steps are slower now, their movements more measured, but the love that binds them remains as strong as ever. Each step proved their years together, the joys, sorrows, laughter, and tears.

They danced on in silence. Their hearts spoke in the quiet intimacy of the moment. They found comfort in the timeless embrace of their love.

Rose and James emerge with a renewed appreciation for each other and the life they've built together. They step off the dance floor, their hands intertwined. They exchanged a loving glance.

"We've been through so much together," she murmured.

James nods, a soft smile gracing his lips. "Here we are, still dancing," he replied, his gaze never leaving hers.

They vow to continue cherishing every moment they have left, finding joy in the simple pleasures of each day and holding onto the remembrances they've created. With each step they take, their connection grows stronger, and their love becomes more resilient.

The dance becomes a bittersweet celebration of their enduring love, a poignant reminder of their journey together. Surrounded by the ghosts of their past and the promise of the future, they overflow with profound gratitude for their life.

Rose's eyes fluttered open. She was lying in bed, the faint morning light filtering through the curtains. She lay there, disoriented, trying to shake off the remnants of the dream that felt so real.

James passed many years ago, leaving behind a void that could never be satisfied.

Tears welled up in Rose's eyes as she clutched the blankets, longing for the warmth of his embrace. Even as she grieved for the loss of her beloved husband, she knew that the encounters they experienced would live on forever in her heart.

Rose's thoughts drifted to James, her heart heavy with the absence of his warm presence beside her. She replayed their dance in the ballroom, the echoes of their laughter, and the whispered promises made under starlit skies.

His presence would always be with her, woven into the fabric of her being. She closed her eyes and vowed to hold onto those memories for as long as she lived, knowing their love would never fade, even through the last dance.

Acknowledgements

Writing a book is never a solitary endeavor, and I am deeply grateful to the incredible individuals who helped shape *Stories from the Heart* into what it is today.

First and foremost, I want to extend my heartfelt thanks to Claire Elisa, Sara Davil, Tiffany Vega, and Lia Thomas. Your insights, feedback, and tireless efforts in shaping these stories and ensuring they were polished to perfection have been invaluable. Your dedication to this project has made all the difference, and I am truly grateful for your contributions.

To my wife, Holli—your love, care, and unwavering support have been the foundation upon which this book was built. Your belief in me and my writing has kept me going, and for that, I am eternally grateful. Thank you for being my rock and my greatest source of inspiration.

Finally, to the readers—thank you from the bottom of my heart. Your willingness to journey through these stories with me means more than words can express. I hope and pray that you find something in these pages that resonates with you, that you see a bit of yourself in the characters, and that the themes of love, resilience, and kindness leave a lasting impact. My greatest hope is that these stories have touched your heart, even just a little and that you carry a piece of them with you as you go.

With gratitude,
John Russell